PSYCHIC SECRET

SAMANTHA BELL

Copyright © 2019 Samantha Bell

All rights reserved.

ISBN: 9781697445404

This is a work of fiction.
Names, characters, businesses, places, events and incidents are either
the products of the author's imagination or used in a fictitious manner.
Any resemblance to actual persons, living or dead,
or actual events is purely coincidental.

Cover art by Danielle Doolitle at DoElle Designs

PSYCHIC SECRET

SAMANTHA BELL

CHAPTER ONE

"Hey, Daniel."

I always knew who was calling before I picked up. It was a neat trick when I was a kid and caller ID wasn't mainstream. Now, no one believed me when I answered my iPhone, because there was no such thing as surprises anymore. My abuela always said that technology took the magic out of life, and while I was grateful for it, sometimes I couldn't help but agree.

"Bianca!" Daniel sounded out of breath. "I'm sorry. Running late. Be there soon."

I peeked into the window of the door leading into our classroom. "No worries, the other group is still trying to sort out some technical difficulties."

"Ok, see you in five!" Daniel hung up.

I pocketed my iPhone and leaned against the wall with a long sigh. I didn't like class presentations and all this waiting had my nerves buzzing. I looked up at the ceiling; the tiles had water stains. Only a few more weeks and I'd be out of here for good. I never liked school very much, much to my parents' disappointment. I had no idea what I was going to do after graduation. I wish I had a plan like Daniel - he was going to State University for forensics.

I told everyone I was taking a gap year to make up my mind, but the closer I got to graduation, the more nervous I became. Everyone was accepted into schools or going backpacking. I would be stuck here in limbo.

A minute later, I heard shoes thumping down the hall. Daniel slid around the corner, clutching his laptop against his chest and his backpack swinging from his other hand. He stopped to catch his breath before giving me a lopsided grin.

"You made it," I said.

"Yep!" Daniel handed me his laptop and our fingers brushed together. He pulled away quickly.

I suppressed a smile. Daniel and I had been best friends since we were kids and I knew he had a huge crush on me, even though he'd never admit it. I liked him too, in a weird way. I just couldn't ever see us dating. He was more like a brother than a boyfriend.

Daniel was a good-looking guy - dark curly brown hair and hazel eyes. He wasn't too tall but taller than me. He had a broad chest and looked stronger than the average nerd, but I didn't think he worked out. He wore square glasses and button-up shirts even in causal situations. He was definitely the kind of guy that you could take to meet your parents.

I turned my head to the sound of clapping from the classroom. "Ok, that would be our cue," I said. "Ready to get this presentation over with?"

∞

"Geez, if I ever have to talk about George Washington again, I think I'll throw up!"

I laughed and nudged Daniel playfully. "Come on, the presentation went great."

"Yeah, but I'm so glad it's over. You know I prefer science over history," He replied before taking a bite of his sandwich.

"I guess so." I looked down at my food, but nothing seemed appetizing. My stomach was still queasy from being in front of the class. Thankfully, I hadn't tripped up on anything I said, and the teacher seemed to like it. I honestly didn't care, as long as I passed.

My other bestie, Jessica, plopped down on the chair across from me. She had art supplies tucked under her arm and was breathing hard. "Oh my God, guys," She breathed. "I seriously don't know how much more of this I can take."

"How much of what?" I asked.

Jessica brushed her chestnut curls out of her face. "The final art project will be the end of me. I've been up until past midnight every day for the past week trying to add finishing touches on my portfolio for college."

"I thought you were accepted?" Daniel asked.

"Conditional acceptance." Jessica cringed. "It's so stressful." She glanced over at my lunch and her eyes perked up. "Are those pupusas? I love your mom's cooking."

I slid the container of cheese-stuffed tortillas over to her. "Knock yourself out. I'm not hungry." I gazed around at the groups of people chattering throughout the cafeteria and was lost to my own anxious thoughts.

∞

Daniel walked me home like he had every day since junior high.

"You doing ok?" He asked after our conversation had faded into silence. "You've seemed kind of down all day. It's not 'cause I was late, was it?"

I shook my head. "No, of course not." I smiled and continued. "I'm fine, really."

Daniel stopped on the sidewalk and put his hand on my shoulder. We were standing in front of my house now. "I know something's not right," He said. "You're my best friend, Bianca. You can tell me."

I sighed. There was no hiding he truth from someone I had known since I was a kid.

"You're right," I admitted. "I'm really worried about what's going to happen after graduation. Everyone else seems to have it all figured out and I'm just going to be left behind."

"Hey, don't think that." Daniel touched my cheek before blushing and pulling his hand away. "I mean, you're a smart girl with so much potential. A gap year is nothing to be ashamed of. Not many people have themselves figured out by the time they're seventeen."

I glanced at my house and then back to him. "What about you?"

Daniel laughed. "I think forensics is the best way for me to get into a job like my dad's. That's why I want to do it." He must have read my mind because he continued. "And Jessica has always been an artist, so it's a no-brainer for her to pursue graphic design."

"I'm just average at everything." I sighed.

"No way!" Daniel protested, looked around and the lowered his voice. "You're the most amazing, kind, intelligent, innovative girl I know. You will find your calling. I know it." He let go of my shoulders. "One day something is going to light a spark in you, and this will all make sense."

I smiled and hugged him. "Thanks, Daniel. You're a good friend."

"I try my best," He said and looked away to disguise how red his face had gotten. "Anyway, I should get going." He motioned down the street toward his own house. "I'll see you tomorrow?"

I nodded. "Sure."

I was almost at the front door when he turned and called back. "Oh, don't forget! The field trip is tomorrow."

I waved in response and let myself in.

My house was nice and well kept, but not too big. A three-bedroom bungalow with two bathrooms and a big office that my parents shared. My dad was an attorney and my mom worked as a freelance Spanish interpreter. She worked from home and my dad commuted downtown. The house was quiet and smelled like coffee, which meant my mother was probably in the office working.

I padded down the hall quietly so I wouldn't disturb her. I passed the first bedroom and felt my chest clench. My abuela had lived with us my entire life and had passed this spring. The hurt was still raw whenever I thought of her. I paused and then pushed the door open. My mother hadn't changed a thing. Her bed was made perfectly, her few clothes and belongings stacked in the closet and a statuette of the Virgin Mary by her bedside. It still smelled like her perfume in here. I rubbed my arms and shivered.

"I miss her too." My mother's voice came from behind me.

I turned around. "Oh, Mama, I'm sorry if I interrupted your work." She must have heard the door open; this room was adjacent to the office.

with thoughts, each more ridiculous than the next. I shrank down into my chair with a shiver.

Mr. Dolinsky sat down across from me. "Just kidding, Bianca," He said. "I got it covered. I'm here to take you home."

"They're letting me go?" I gasped.

"This investigation has been taken over by the FBI," He said with a smirk.

"Do cops really hate you guys as much as they do on TV?"

Mr. Dolinsky let out a loud laugh. "Sometimes, yeah, they do." He stood and pocketed his badge. "Come on, your mother is worried sick."

I walked straight out of the office with him leading the way. I caught a glimpse at the "bad cop" who scowled. He looked like a kid who lost his favorite toy. I ignored him, keeping my eyes straight at the back of Mr. Dolinsky. He stopped only once to sign out and then I was free.

The evening air seemed sweet. I took a deep breath and smiled.

Mr. Dolinsky's black car was parked outside. He opened the door for me. "After you," He said.

"Thanks." I looked over my shoulder at the police office one more time before sliding into the car. "Thanks for getting me out of there," I said once the office was out of view.

"No problem, Bianca. I have to look out for Daniel's friends," He said. "Sorry that you got caught up in that situation at the Institute." He glanced at me quickly when he stopped at a red light. "Do you know exactly what happened?"

I stiffened. I wasn't prepared for more questioning.

"Off the record, of course," Mr. Dolinsky added. "I'm not talking to you as FBI right now. I just want to make sure that you are ok. Daniel already told me what happened, but I'd like to hear your side of the story."

"Off the record?" I repeated.

"Promise," He replied.

I let out a sigh as he drove towards the freeway. "Alright," I conceded. "Well, the whole situation was really weird. I heard some noises in a closed exhibit and you know how I am with being curious." He chuckled, and I relaxed a bit more. "So anyway, there was some guy in there looking for something. There were lots of boxes of jewelry and stuff. It was a mess."

"What happened next?"

I took a deep breath. In all the commotion, I barely had time to register what I saw earlier that day. It seemed like a dream. I continued, unable to believe what I was saying. "Well, the guy was really weird. He did something and all the crates of jewelry rose up and flew everywhere. Then they caught on fire. After that he must have escaped, but the door was locked behind us." I shivered. "It was awful."

My mother shook her head and put a hand on my shoulder. "Not at all. Let's have some coffee."

I let her lead me to the kitchen where she prepared fresh coffee and cookies for a snack. I watched her work in the kitchen like a machine, knowing where everything was without even having to think about it.

My mind began to wander, and I glanced into the living room. My favorite family photo hung on the wall. It was of my parents, abuela, and me.

My mother's family had fled El Salvador during the 1980s. She met my father when they were both attending Purdue University; he was studying law, and she was studying modern languages. They got married and settled down in Michigan after they graduated. My abuela fell ill after the death of her husband and she moved in with them. They adopted me a year later.

I looked nothing like my parents; my father was Mexican American and my mother from El Salvador. I was pale, with almond eyes and dark, straight hair. My birth mother was Korean, but I didn't know much more than that. I never thought of it anyway, because my true family was here. I had no brothers or sisters, but my family ties were strong.

My mother set down a steaming cup of black coffee in front of me. "What's bothering you, mi cielito?"

I had been through my worries what seemed like a million times already today. I sighed. "Just worried about what to do after graduation."

She sipped her coffee and gave me a knowing smile with a twinkle in her eye. "You'll figure it out," She said. "Just because the world is moving fast, doesn't mean you need to try to catch up to it. Everything at your own pace. You'll be fine."

∞

Afterward, I headed up to my room to prepare for the field trip tomorrow. I wasn't exactly thrilled about going to an art museum, but anything was better than having to sit through an afternoon of boring classes.

I felt a strange yet familiar tingle and glanced down at my phone. It felt as if someone would call me, but the screen remained blank. I frowned and shrugged it off.

"One day something is going to light a spark in you, and this will all make sense."

Daniels words floated through my head again. Maybe I was just losing my mind, but I had a funny feeling about tomorrow.

CHAPTER TWO

"Welcome to the Detroit Institute of Arts," Our guide rambled on about the history of the building we were standing in. "The Institute was founded in 1885, but was moved to this site in 1927."

I fidgeted, already growing restless in the cold room as the echoes of voices and footsteps filled my ears. I glanced over at Jessica, who was absorbing everything the guide said. Her eyes were wide, so big she almost looked like an alien. I suppressed a giggle.

"I wish I was that passionate about old stuff," Daniel whispered to me as we watched Jessica wriggle her way to the front of the crowd.

"You're that passionate about science stuff," I countered. "You and her are really just two sides of the same coin."

Daniel shrugged.

We trailed behind the rest of the group. We were supposed to be taking notes for an essay after the visit, but I just snapped pictures with my iPhone camera instead.

Daniel shoved his hands in his pockets and walked lazily around, looking at the paintings. I followed him, thankful there was someone as disenchanted here as me. Our teacher and the guide were talking animatedly and most of the other students were consumed in the art.

Part of me felt bad. I mean, I should love the history and beauty around me, but something else was hanging over my head. I couldn't quite place it. The eerie feeling that I had felt yesterday was returning.

Then, something caught my attention. Out of the corner of my eye I saw a shadowy figure slip through the hallway. I stopped and blinked. It must have been my imagination. People don't creep around art galleries in the middle of the day. I looked over my shoulder, but the guide had continued on into the next room with the group of students following like hypnotized zombies.

I couldn't shake the feeling. With one more glance I checked to make sure I wasn't being followed and then slunk off in the direction of the shadowy person.

The long marble hallway led to a heavy wooden door. There was a velvet rope across it and a sign that read: *EXHIBIT CLOSED*.

I paused and took a step back. My curiosity always got the best of me. How many times had I gotten mixed up because I just couldn't help myself? Like when we were kids, Daniel and I went exploring a construction site and I twisted my ankle in a pot hole; or last year when Jessica and I pretended we were going to a sleep over and instead went to a college house party that had to get broken up by the cops?

There was a sound from the other side. Something metal falling to the floor. The clatter echoed.

I should have known better, but yet again, I didn't listen to that voice inside my head. I sucked in a breath and placed my hand on the doorknob.

"Bianca," Daniel whispered.

I turned around. Daniel was coming down the hall. "Oh," I said let go of the handle as if it had burned me. "What's up? I got separated from the group."

"I was coming to look for you." He stopped a pace away from me. "Are you ok?"

I opened my mouth to reply when another crash echoed from behind the door. We both spun around.

"What was that?" He asked.

"I don't know," I reached for the door again. "That's what I was checking out."

Daniel didn't hesitate. He lifted the velvet rope. "Let's go see but be careful. Might be a thief or something."

"In the middle of the day?"

Daniel shrugged. "Hey, my dad works for the FBI remember? I've heard stranger stories that that."

"What do we do if it is a thief?" I whispered.

Daniel held up his phone. "911 is always the best choice." He grinned.

I nodded, slipped under the rope and twisted the knob. I was half expecting it to be locked, so when the heavy wooden door opened, I let out a gasp.

The room was dark inside. I peered into the gap and saw nothing but darkness. I looked back at Daniel, who gave me a reassuring nod and we entered. It took a moment for my eyes to adjust to the dark. I held my phone in front of me, using the flashlight to look around.

The room was nearly empty. There was a thick layer of dust on the floor and tables.

Daniel directed the light from his phone to the floor. There were footprints in the dust. "Ah ha," He breathed. "I've found a clue."

I rolled my eyes. "You read too much *Sherlock*," I said.

Daniel shrugged my sarcastic remark off and looked around. "Well, whoever it was, I guess they're gone now."

I shone the flashlight on the walls. There were framed paintings dotted randomly and empty hardware in between. The room was small, probably for private events or something like that. But now, it just looked like it was used for storage.

There was a metallic sound of something falling to the floor. Daniel and I both twisted around to a stack of crates against the far wall. Something glittered in the light from our phones. The weird feeling surged through me again. Whatever it was, I had to have it.

I stepped forward, but Daniel caught my hand. "Come on, I think we should go and report this to security."

"Getting cold feet already?" I teased. He had matured since our childhood adventures, but I didn't expect him to back out now. "I just want to see what it is."

"I don't think we're alone in here." Daniel whispered.

That got my attention. I held my breath, listening for any sound of movement. He was right; stuff didn't fall out of boxes on its own.

A shadow edged across my vision again. Muted sounds of careful footsteps came from the far wall.

I summoned my courage and shouted. "Who's there?"

Daniel hissed in my ear. "Don't do that, that's how people die in horror movies."

The crates fell in a crash. Antique jewelry and packing foam tumbled out in a wave. A figure dressed in black stepped out from behind the mess. Whoever he was, he was breathing hard and looked very angry.

Daniel and I stepped back. He threw his arm in front of me and tapped the emergency dial on his cell phone.

"911, what's your emergency?" The operator responded after one ring.

"We're at the Detroit Institute of Art, there's a break in." Daniel barked. "Send police. Hurry!"

The man in darkness laughed. "No need, I already have what I came for, children." He held up something shiny.

I felt the tug again, but I could barely make out what he had in his hand. If I had to guess, it looked like a necklace. "No, stop!" I cried.

The man cackled and swung his arm through the air. I didn't believe what I saw next. The boxes raised up from the ground, raining gold and precious metals. There was a low frequency hum, and they burst into flames.

I shrieked.

Daniel pushed me back towards the door. "Let's get out of here!"

"No!" I pulled away from him. "I need that thing!"

The room was hot and filled with smoke. The man had disappeared, but how? The only way out was the door behind us.

"Leave it!" Daniel obviously had no idea what I was freaking out about. "Come on, let's go." He tugged on the doorknob, but it was locked. The door must have locked from the outside. We were trapped.

I swallowed the bile that rose in my throat. "Oh no, we can't get out." I screamed. The smoke was burning my eyes. The fire licked the tables and traveled up the heavy curtains that covered the windows.

Daniel was shouting something, probably to the 911 operator.

My heart was pounding so loud that it filled my ears. I couldn't hear anything and despite the stench of smoke and the heat of the fire, I suddenly felt very calm. I raised my arms, splayed my hands wide and felt a surge of adrenaline. There was an odd hum, one that could be felt more than heard.

I snapped my eyes open and everything around us shattered. The windows against the far wall blew out one by one sending shards of glass raining down, the picture frames broke, and the few remaining boxes exploded with their precious contents flying about the room. The giant wooden door groaned and buckled, falling outward into the hallway.

I could hear the sounds of sirens in the distance. The fire alarm rang out through the building and the sprinkler system finally kicked on. The cool water rained down on us just as the police came running in.

I swayed on my feet, suddenly overcome with exhaustion. My eyes locked on to Daniel and then I fainted.

CHAPTER THREE

"Young lady, I need to contact your parents," The doctor said to me.

I shook my head. I hated the feeling of the oxygen mask on my face. "My dad is at a conference out of state and my mom will worry, please, I'm fine." I pulled my mask off so my voice wouldn't be muffled.

The doctor pressed his lips together and he stood up stiffly. "You do know there are police waiting to speak to you, right?"

I blinked and bolted up from the hospital bed. Two policemen stood by the door. One had his arms crossed and was staring at me, while the other was working on the report. "I'm *fine*," I said again, with emphasis.

The doctor rolled his eyes and walked away. "Kids," I heard him mutter under his breath. He moved on to the next room, shouting about insurance or something to one of the nurses.

The cops shut the door behind them and sat down on either side of the bed.

"Ms. Hernandez," One officer said and then looked down to double check the form.

I ignored it, I was used to people thinking my name and my face didn't match up.

"You and Daniel Dolinsky were found at a crime scene this afternoon and are under the suspicion of arson," The officer continued.

"Daniel!" I gasped. "Where is he? Is he ok?"

The second cop spoke. "Being treated for smoke inhalation but expected to be fine. You're both very lucky."

The first cop cleared his throat and continued. "We're going to have to ask you a few questions, miss."

Now it was my turn to look tough, despite an oxygen mask dangling from my neck. "I won't speak without my lawyer."

∞

Not many girls my age knew much about the legal system. Every summer for the past three years I worked at my dad's office filling in for vacation times so the receptionists and assistants could have a break. It was mostly mind-numbing clerical work like getting coffee, photocopying or data entry, but I had learned a thing or two over the past few years.

The cops had left me alone in an interrogation room. I was happy they were gone. The taller of the two had the whole "bad cop" thing going on, while the other looked distinctly uncomfortable with the entire situation.

When I refused to talk, the jerk cop stormed out and his partner followed.

I too a sip of water from the bottle they had put in front of me. I was beyond thirsty, but I didn't want them to see me weak. One drop renewed my thirst and I downed the rest of it without stopping for a breath.

The door opened and I looked up. To my surprise, it was neither the good cop or the bad cop or a lawyer. It was Daniel's father. "Mr. Dolinsky?" I gasped.

Aaron Dolinsky, aka Mr. D, aka Daniel's dad, was a tall, muscular man with the same curly hair and hazel eyes. His short beard was speckled with gray to match his temples. He looked exactly what I figured Daniel would look like in thirty years. He was dressed in plain civilian clothes. His FBI badge was in his hand.

He grinned; it was the same crooked grin that Daniel had. "I told you to call me Aaron," He said. Then his expression turned cold and steely. He threw down his badge on the table. "But right now, I suppose, it's Inspector."

I felt the blood drain from my face. The FBI wanted me now? No way. Wasn't this a conflict of interest anyway? My mind flooded

Mr. Dolinsky nodded. "Then what happened?"

"Daniel called 911," I said. I hesitated, not sure if I should admit to what happened next. How had I broken those windows? Was it really me or was it from the heat of the fire? I doubted everything now.

I glanced at Daniel's dad who was waiting patiently for me to continue. If Daniel had already told his side of the story, did he already know about whatever the heck happened with me? Whatever. I needed to tell someone, may as well be Inspector Dolinsky. "Then I'm not really sure what happened," I said, and it was the truth. "I felt really weird and then all the windows shattered. The sprinklers turned on and I fainted."

Mr. Dolinsky nodded. "Yes, that's what Daniel said too."

I breathed a sigh of relief. Then I wasn't crazy. Thank goodness. "I don't remember anything that happened after that. I woke up in the hospital and then was taken in by the police."

There was silence as we drove until reaching my house. Mr. Dolinsky parked the car and then turned to face me. "Listen, Bianca, I know this was a really weird night for you, but I need you to promise that you won't mention any of the strange events to your parents. They were only told about the fire, nothing more."

I nodded, swallowing the lump in my throat. "Alright," I said. I wasn't going to argue with an FBI inspector. "But, why?"

"It's classified."

I nodded again.

"I want you to meet me tomorrow morning at my house. Just tell your mom that you're studying or something."

I raised my eyebrows. Mr. Dolinsky knew as well as my mother did that, I would never get up early on a Saturday morning to study.

"Or, shopping then," He laughed.

"Alright." I reached for the door handle. "Anything else?"

"Yeah," Mr. Dolinsky said, almost as an afterthought. "Until the investigation is over, I need you to promise you won't tell anyone about we talk about."

I nodded.

"Bianca, you're psychic."

CHAPTER FOUR

How was I supposed to sleep after that?

I lay awake in bed, staring at the ceiling and counting the minutes until morning. What kind of person drops a bomb like "you're psychic" and then leaves the explanation for another day? It was like a bad cliff hanger.

I rolled over and closed my eyes. Daniel's father promised it would all make sense in the morning. Maybe I was just going crazy. A mental breakdown was much easier to consider than the fact that Mr. Dolinsky thought I had some supernatural psychic powers. I was no expert, but I was pretty sure that was against the laws of science or something.

I needed a better explanation than that and I was going to get it at dawn.

The sun was barely over the horizon when I pounded on the Dolinsky's front door. The air was heavy with dew and the entire neighborhood was quiet.

As expected, I hadn't slept a wink. I waited until six in the morning, tip-toed out of the house, and ran straight to the place where I would get answers.

I knocked again, even louder than last time. The sound echoed through the cul-de-sac, but I didn't care who I woke up.

The door opened a minute later. It was Daniel's father, Inspector Dolinsky, dressed in a robe and holding a giant mug of black coffee.

He rubbed his eyes and looked down at me. "Bianca, when I said the morning..."

"No. I want answers now." I interrupted and brushed past him. "I'm not leaving until you tell me what really happened yesterday," I paused and then added, "Please."

Mr. Dolinsky sighed and took a swig of coffee. "Fine," He said. "I suppose I owe you that much." He motioned to the living room. "Go have a seat. I need to make more coffee."

I went to the living room to wait.

Nothing had changed since Daniel's parents got divorced a few years ago. Mrs. Dolinsky had been the one to decorate and take care of the house. Judging by the dust on the shelves, no one else cared much. I sat down on the green couch that looked like something my grandmother would have picked out in the

1990s. The brass clock on the wall ticked ominously in the silence.

I sat with my arms crossed over my chest until Mr. Dolinsky returned.

He came back a few minutes later, dressed in a t-shirt and jeans and two cups of coffee. He set one down in front of me before taking a sip of his. "So," He said as he sat down across from me. "What do you want to know?"

"Where do I start?" I stammered. "You dropped me off last night after some crazy ordeal and then go: *Oh, but the way, you're a wizard, Harry!*" I did a terrible Hagrid impression.

Mr. Dolinsky laughed. "No, not a wizard. Psychic."

"Yeah, that."

The man sighed and looked past me across the room. "I'm not sure where to start."

"Anywhere," I pleaded.

"Alright," He shrugged. "Well, you know I work for the FBI. What very few people know is that I work for a division of the FBI that deals with unexplainable events."

"Like UFOs?"

"No, they have a different department for that," Mr. Dolinsky said almost too casually. "Anyway. I work with people like you. People with powers that seem to defy science and reason. The government has been involved for the past several decades to ensure that we keep the public safe."

"Safe? From psychic people?"

"Yep." He nodded. "If people like you don't learn to control their powers, it can be very dangerous."

"People like me," I whispered. I closed my eyes and took a deep breath.

"I know this is hard to believe," Mr. Dolinsky continued as if he could read my mind.

"No kidding!" I slumped back against the couch.

There were a few moments of silence. The only sound was the clock ticking on the wall. Finally, Mr. Dolinsky spoke again. "I know this is hard," He repeated. "But we have measures in place. Policies. Best practices. It won't be so bad."

I looked at him as he sipped his coffee. Mine was going cold on the table. "Why me?"

Mr. Dolinsky raised his eyebrows. "Why you? Why anyone?" He shrugged. "Despite advances in technology and research, we know very little about this phenomenon."

"What do I do now?"

"For the moment just hang tight." Mr. Dolinsky said. "I need to contact some people and get everything in order."

"Hang tight?" I shook my head and let out a cynical laugh. "You mean, just go back to normal like I'm not some freak? How do I know any of this is real? Is it a joke?" I felt energy raising inside of me. "I don't want this. I didn't ask for it. I just want to graduate high school!"

The wave of energy rippled inside of me with the same low hum.

"Bianca, I need you to relax." Mr. Dolinsky's voice was calm and even.

His calmness irritated me. "How can I relax?" I asked. "How can I even believe anything you say?" I let out a gasp, fighting back frustrated tears.

Suddenly, the mug of coffee in front of me rose from the table. It cracked and shattered, sending ceramic and coffee flying in a circle.

My lips trembled. "No. This can't be real."

"It is real, Bianca," Mr. Dolinsky ignored the coffee seeping into the plush carpet and the shards of ceramic scattered around the living room. "I promise this will make sense soon. It might take a little while, but you'll learn to live with it."

"Is everything ok, Dad?" Daniel appeared at the foot of the staircase. His brow furrowed when he saw the mess. His eyes flicked from his father to my tear-stained face. "What's going on?"

"Nothing," Mr. Dolinsky said in a tone that assured no follow up questions would be asked.

I suddenly felt very sick. I blinked and swallowed hard, but my vision kept fading in and out. Exhaustion was consuming me. Strangling me. My body was so weak. Why hadn't I slept? I looked from Daniel to his father.

"I don't feel so well," I muttered.

Daniel caught me as I fell forward from the couch and helped me lay down. I didn't miss the look he shot his dad before going to get a towel to clean up the coffee.

"Using your power will drain your energy. That's why you fainted yesterday," Mr. Dolinsky said once Daniel was out of earshot. "You didn't sleep last night?"

I shook my head.

Mr. Dolinsky sighed. "Let's get you home so you can rest. In the meantime, try to avoid any outbursts like that. Now that your powers have awakened, you need to remain as calm as possible until we get things sorted out."

"Sorted out?" I asked.

He nodded. "I will be in touch soon. There's a program in place to help young psychics after their talents activate. Once I make a few calls, we'll have answers." Mr. Dolinsky said. "To be honest, I've never been around when someone activates. I'm normally involved much later down the line. So, please be patient with me."

Mr. Dolinsky helped me to my feet. He touched my shoulder and looked at me straight. "Listen, Bianca. I've known you since you were a little girl with lopsided pigtails and braces. You're like a daughter to me. Trust me, I will do everything in my power to get you the help you need."

I was lying on my bed and staring at my ceiling when my phone buzzed. It was another missed call from Daniel.

I left the Dolinsky's house without saying goodbye to him; his father hadn't tried to stop me when I pulled on my shoes and ran back home. I couldn't bear to hear another word about this world that I'd suddenly been thrust into.

Daniel had called nearly a dozen times in the paste few hours. Did he know what I was? How much of the conversation did he hear? Did his father tell him the truth? No doubt he thought I was some freak now.

I stared at my hands, letting them go in and out of focus. I opened and closed them, rubbed my palms together, and flexed my fingers. The low pulse of energy did not return. Did it only work when I was angry or in danger? Or was I hallucinating this whole thing? For all I knew, I might still be in the hospital in a coma or something.

I sighed, flicking my hands towards the ceiling one more time before giving up. I let my arms fall to my sides.

Exhaustion was creeping through my body again. I needed sleep more than anything right now. I closed my eyes and exhaled. I burrowed into my warm blankets and my body slowly began to relax. My tense, knotted muscles became limp and my breath slowed.

I surrendered to sleep. Maybe once I woke up everything would go back to normal.

CHAPTER FIVE

It was dark when my eyes opened again. The light in the hallway was on; I could see my mother's shadow as she paced. She was on the phone to my father, speaking Spanish so quickly I could barely understand her in my groggy state.

There was a big glass of water by my bed. She must have come in to check on me.

I bolted up and downed the water greedily, not noticing how thirsty I was until I saw it.

"Yes, she's been sleeping for over twelve hours." My mother whispered. Her shadow drifted away as she walked towards her office. Her voice faded and I heard a door click shut.

I glanced at my clock. It was past midnight. I finally felt rested but now I was starving. It was a deep hunger that clawed at my insides as if I hadn't eaten in days. I collapsed back into my bed and checked my phone.

15 missed calls: Daniel

So many missed calls. Two voice mails and too many texts to count. The last text was from ten minutes ago: *Bianca, please say something. I'm worried.*

I sighed.

Before I could reply I heard a tapping on my window. I bolted up and pulled back my curtains.

"Daniel?" I gasped.

My best friend was grinning, leaning against the roof. There was a perfectly placed tree near that side of my house and the slanted roof made getting in and out of my room easy. How many times had I snuck out of the window when I was younger? I had lost count.

I opened the window and popped out the screen. I was an expert at this.

Daniel slipped in and smiled. "Bianca."

I didn't hesitate; I pulled him into a tight hug. "I'm sorry I didn't message you back. I was sleeping."

Daniel chuckled. "Now that's a familiar excuse."

"It's true," I whispered.

"I know. That ordeal yesterday must have really drained you, huh?" Daniel smiled.

I sighed. "Yeah." Maybe his father hadn't told him anything. Maybe he hadn't heard anything. That was the only way our friendship would be normal now. I wanted to tell him the truth so badly, but how would he take it? I barely could grasp it myself. How could he believe me when I didn't even believe it?

Daniel broke away from the hug. "Hey, if you want to talk, we should probably get out." He nodded his head towards the window.

I glanced over my shoulder. The hallway light was off now. My mother must have finally gone to sleep. "Alright."

I threw on a hoodie and gathered my long black hair into a ponytail. I looked back over my shoulder one last time, slipped on some flip-flops and then followed Daniel out into the night.

Daniel climbed down the tree with surprising ease. I didn't miss how his muscles flexed underneath his gray t-shirt. The glow from the streetlight cast shadows on his face and body. I ignored the spark of attraction burning in my chest.

"Hey, I meant to ask, have you been working out or something?" I asked as I hopped down from the lowest branch.

Daniel looked away and shoved his hands into his pockets. "Yeah, a bit," He admitted. "Just cause I'm going into a white-collar industry, doesn't mean that my health has to suffer."

I smiled. He was really taking college seriously. I was both proud and jealous. Only a few days ago, I wished desperately that I had college figured out and now I would have given anything to feel that normal again.

"So, you hungry?" Daniel asked.

"Starving!" I exclaimed.

Daniel laughed. "Well come on, let's grab something to eat. My treat."

We both knew that the only thing open in our neighborhood at this time was the 7-11 a few blocks away. I didn't care. I piled two hot dogs with nacho cheese and olives, a Big Gulp full of Sprite and a bag of candy.

Daniel and I sat on the curb while I ate. He watched me, smirking. "Wow, you weren't lying when you said you were hungry."

I wiped some cheese from my lip. "I'm sorry," I laughed.

"Don't be," Daniel handed me a napkin. "I think I'm the only guy in the world that you'd be comfortable enough with to eat a nacho-cheese hot dog with." He wrinkled his nose. "With olives."

I giggled and tossed an olive at him.

Daniel dodged out of the way. "Gross! I don't know how you can eat those."

"Everything tastes delicious." I said after taking a big sip of Sprite.

"You know those hot dogs might have been sitting there since last Tuesday."

I rolled my eyes. "Doubt it. And even if they were, I'd chance it."

We both laughed.

The silence settled around us and was only broken by the sound of Daniel's slushy. He twisted the straw around in the cup. He cleared his throat before speaking. "So, I guess it's true that people are really hungry and tired after having an... episode."

I sputtered and choked on my drink. "What?"

"I mean, psychic people."

I froze. My hand was shaking as I clutched the Big Gulp tightly.

Daniel turned to look at me fully. "Please don't be upset. I didn't mean it in a bad way," He added hurriedly. "I've just never really known a psychic. Well, besides my dad but that doesn't count."

"Your dad?" My voice squeaked. Mr. Dolinsky was a psychic too? How could he not have told me?

Daniel nodded.

A car pulled into the parking lot and shone its headlights in our direction. We both blinked and turned away from the blinding light. A middle-aged woman with auburn-red got out of the car and strode into the store. She made an annoyed sound in our direction, probably thinking we were some good-for-nothing hoodlums. The bell chimed as the door closed behind her.

"Come on," Daniel said. "We probably shouldn't be talking here anyway."

∞

Daniel and I went to the park. It was small and shielded by trees. No one would be out at this time of night and it was secluded enough that no one should overhear our conversation. We sat on the swings like we used to do when we were kids.

"So, you know about psychics?" I asked.

Daniel nodded. "Yeah, my dad told me about them after he and Mom got divorced. I know he works for the special FBI division. But that's about it. It's pretty much on a need-to-know basis. Mom left him because he had to keep so many secrets. She said she couldn't trust him anymore." His voice drifted away.

"Oh, I see." I hadn't ever asked about the details of the divorce. It always seemed like such an awkward topic and I was no good with those. I hadn't even been able to talk properly at my abuela's funeral.

Daniel shrugged. "Whatever." He looked up at the sky and leaned back a little. "We're not here to talk about that, anyway."

"So, you're not weirded out by this?" I asked.

"You being psychic?" Daniel laughed. "No way! This is great actually." He paused. "Well, maybe not for you but for me it's cool. You'll be ok, Bianca. I'm glad my dad found out so he can help you."

I nodded. "Yeah, at least there's that."

"You don't sound very excited," Daniel said as he pushed off from the swing. He stood in front of me, his face breaking into a huge smile. "I mean, I know if I suddenly found out I had awesome powers, I'd be stoked!"

I laughed weakly.

"I'm serious!" He insisted.

"It's not like a comic book, Daniel," I sighed. "I'm just so confused. I don't even know what my powers do or how to make them work. Your dad said to be patient, but it's been twenty-four hours and I have no answers."

Daniel shoved his hands in his pockets. "Yeah, I guess you're right. But every great hero has an origin story!"

I laughed and shook my head. "Again with the superhero talk?"

Daniel shrugged. "Well, I know it's not exactly like that..." He trailed off and then gasped. "Come on, why don't we practice a little and see what you can do?"

My mouth went dry. "Are you serious?"

Daniel nodded. "Yeah, why not?"

I stood and looked at my hands. I opened and closed them, but no low hum came. There was no feeling of energy rising through me. I felt completely normal. "I don't know how to summon it," I said. "The last two times I just got emotional and then it happened."

"Let's give it a shot," Daniel said. His positivity might just start wearing off on me soon.

I sighed and rolled my shoulders. "Alright, I'll try for you."

Daniel grinned and looked around. He found an empty pop can and placed it on the ground in front of me. "So, your powers are telekinetic right?"

"Telekinetic?" I repeated.

"Yeah, like you can move stuff with your mind."

"I guess so. I mean, so far I've only broken stuff."

Daniel nodded at the can. "You can do it. This one isn't glass so maybe it'll work better."

I held out my hand and then hesitated. "How do you know all this stuff?"

"Internet research," Daniel replied with a shrug. "Once I knew that psychic abilities were actually real, a deep web search revealed the rest. I just couldn't talk about it with anyone until now. I didn't want anyone to think I was crazy."

"Maybe we're both just crazy," I laughed.

I flexed my hands again and exhaled. This was insane. I stared at the can, but nothing happened. Not even the smallest twitch. No low humming feeling. No energy. I sighed and threw my hands up in the air. "This isn't working!"

"Be patient," Daniel insisted.

I clenched my teeth and balled my fists. Easy for him to say. He wasn't the one who recently discovered they were some sort of scientific freak. I blew out a breath and tried again, but nothing came without emotion.

"I don't think I can do this," I said finally.

Daniel looked up and his face went pale. "Bianca, behind you!"

My mouth went dry and my body buzzed with energy. "What?" I threw up my hands and whirled around to see nothing. I blinked, and the can came soaring down from above me, bouncing a few feet away. I looked down at my hands. "Did I do that?"

"Yep! Sorry I had to scare you to make it happen," Daniel said.

We both looked at the deformed can. The hum was still present in my body. I grasped the feeling desperately and reached out towards the lump of aluminum. I flexed my fingers and saw the can twitch. I gasped and concentrated harder. There was a pause and then the can flew up over our heads again and landed in the grass.

"You did it!" Daniel gasped.

"Yeah, I did!" I looked down at my hands, unable to believe it. The hum was fading again. The low frequency sound rumbled through me. It started in my head and traveled down my spine, curling out like roots throughout my entire body. I suddenly felt very tired.

Daniel caught me as I stumbled. "Bianca!" He helped me sit on the grass. "Here, you should rest."

I lay back in the grass, ignoring the dampness and shaking away the thought of any spiders or crickets might be lurking there. I was too exhausted to let that bother me. It wasn't as bad as the last two times, but the drain on my body was undeniable.

Suddenly, a chill blew though the park. I bolted up and looked around. "What was that?"

"What was what?" Daniel asked.

"You didn't feel that cold?" I asked.

My friend shook his head. "No, come on, we'd better get you home."

"She won't be going home tonight, nerd." A raspy voice came from above us.

I looked up to see a man hovering at the tree line. He was dressed in black, standing casually, and he might have looked normal if he hadn't been standing on thin air. He looked down at us with a grin.

I shrank back. This wasn't the same person who we saw at the museum, but at least now I knew what we were dealing with. Another psychic.

"She'll be coming with me," The man said.

"Like hell she will!" Daniel threw his arm in front of me and helped me get to my feet. My body was weak, and my legs trembled. I was grateful for his strength. I clutched his shoulder to keep myself standing.

"Daniel, he's psychic too," I whispered. "We can't do anything against him."

Daniel clenched his teeth. "Hold on, I'll think of something." He held his breath, probably racking his memory for anything helpful he had found on the deep web.

The man raised his hand, and the trees groaned. The wood bent to his will and the wind picked up. "Fine. I'll get rid of you, little boy, and then I'll take my prize." His dark eyes locked onto mine and I wished I hadn't wasted my energy on that can.

The trees creaked and rustled as they bowed to the man's powers. He laughed manically and flexed his hands. As he thrust his arms upward, the trees groaned, and the wind whipped around us. The wind howled like a demon.

"We have to get out of here," I shouted. My hair flew into my mouth and eyes. My voice was barely audible over the wind. I gripped Daniel's hand.

The ground beneath us shifted, and we were flung like toys onto the grass.

I groaned as pain shot through my body. Whoever this guy was, I didn't want to mess with him. Daniel helped me up again and we began to back away.

The man leered at us. "What? Going so soon? Don't you want to have some fun?" He cackled.

Suddenly, something dark flew out of the trees and struck the man. He was sent crashing to the ground. The wind stopped. Two boys appeared they were probably about my age. One was pale with blond hair and the other was dark-skinned with hair cut short to his skull. They were tall, dressed in black, and very threatening.

The dark-skinned boy dropped to the grass on one knee. He was panting hard, but a focused light gleamed in his eyes.

The pale boy stood with twin daggers in his hands. He glanced at Daniel and me. Our eyes locked, and I felt a shiver run down my spine. His blue eyes were like ice. He smirked at me and I felt a slight pain in my head.

I groaned and looked away, covering my eyes with my hand. The energy in my body flexed, but nothing happened. I was still too weak.

The man struggled to his feet and snarled at the boys. "Stay out of this, academy scum!" He shouted. Spit flew from his mouth. He held out his hands and the wind surged forward, but he was no match for the other two.

The pale boy flicked his hands down and the daggers extended like switchblades.

"Come on, Bianca, we should go." Daniel whispered to me. He helped me to my feet, but I could not tear my eyes away from the fight.

"We can't leave them like this," I said.

"Pretty sure they can take care of themselves," Daniel replied.

As if to prove Daniel's point, the boys lunged at the man. The dark boy faded in and out of sight. He disappeared and reappeared behind the man. The pale boy lashed out with one of his blades, catching the man in the arm.

The wind howled in response.

"We need to disable his power!" One of them yelled over the blast.

The man vanished, just missing another attack. He reappeared above the trees and let out a laugh. "You think you preppy boys can handle me?" He grinned. There was a rumble from beneath us and the ground began to shake.

"Shit, he's strong." The blond boy said. He adjusted his stance and held up his daggers.

The two worked together as a team, but I could sense just the smallest hint of tension between them. Obviously, this rivalry had to be put aside to defeat the common enemy, but it was still noticeable.

The pair clashed against the man again. He fell to the ground. The rumbling feeling returned but it was weaker this time. It sputtered and began to fade.

"Now, while he's weak!" The pale boy shouted.

As they both lunged in attack the man threw up his arms and disappeared into thin air.

"Shit!" The blond one exclaimed and kicked the ground.

They spoke to each other. It was too quiet for me to catch, but their faces looked serious and concerned. As if sensing my gaze, they turned towards me.

Daniel tensed defensively. Were they friends or foes?

"Tell no one what you saw." A voice filled my head. I heard it as plain as if it were someone talking right in front of me. I knew it came from one of them, but who? How had they entered my mind like that? Energy pulsed through the air and the voice was gone.

The two boys stared at me for a long moment. The silence crushed me. Without a word, the dark-skinned boy grabbed his partner's forearm, and they vanished without a trace.

∞

Daniel walked me home in shocked silence.

I was tired and weak, clinging to the arm of his sweater to keep my balance.

We stopped at the tree under my window and both looked up. "Now would be a good time to know how to teleport, right?" I joked.

Daniel shook his head and smiled. "You know, when I found out about my dad's powers, I was jealous. Now it seems that maybe they're too draining on the system to be worth it." He shrugged. "Come on. I'll give you a boost."

I used Daniel's shoulders to climb up into the tree and to the window. "Thanks," I whispered and waved.

Daniel waved back before taking off. The last thing we needed was for my mother to wake up and find us sneaking back in. I had worried her enough for one day.

I shrugged off my clothes and collapsed into bed. My body was aching and numb, but my mind was going a mile a minute. I tried to process everything that happened tonight, but I couldn't find the words to describe what I had seen. It was bizarre.

I let out a long sigh. My chest ached. Abuela would have been perfect to talk to right now; she would have understood. I missed her so much. Blinking away tears, I rolled over and shut my eyes. My only hope now was that Mr. Dolinsky would have answers for me in the morning.

CHAPTER SIX

Monday morning, I took a detour on the way to school and met Mr. Dolinsky. He was parked a block away from the school, as he promised he would be.

I told him everything about what had happened in the park; I could barely believe the words that were coming out of my mouth. I would have thought it was crazy if I hadn't seen it with my own eyes. Psychic people. Fighting. Different powers. It was like something out of a TV show, but it wasn't. Was this really going to be my life now?

Mr. Dolinsky nodded. "I'm glad you told me. I have made preparations for you today. Hopefully we can get you under protection and you won't need to worry about Rogues anymore."

"Rogues?" I asked.

Mr. Dolinsky nodded. "Some psychics refuse to cooperate with the government. They go into crime and use their powers for evil. They're always trying to recruit new blood before the FBI can get to them. They must have sensed your powers awaken. That's why that guy followed you to the park last night."

I swallowed hard. "I thought he was trying to kill me."

Mr. Dolinsky shook his head. He turned the key in the ignition, and we made our way towards the highway. Thankfully, the windows were tinted so no one would catch me skipping school.

"He wouldn't kill you. He was only trying to capture you," Mr. Dolinsky said. "Psychic blood is hard to find these days. We're a dying breed."

"We're?" I repeated in surprise. I didn't want him to know that his son had already told me.

Mr. Dolinsky nodded. "Yes, me too. That's how I got involved with the FBI. But my powers are passive and not exactly helpful for much on the front lines." He laughed and shook his head. "I guess I should be thankful for that."

"What is your talent?" I asked.

He glanced at me before returning his attention to the road. "Just typical clairvoyance. It comes in handy during investigations."

Clairvoyance seemed far from typical to me. I slumped back into the seat and adjusted the seatbelt that was digging into my neck. "So that's how you knew how to find us every time Jessica, Daniel, and I went out past curfew."

Mr. Dolinsky laughed. "Sometimes. Other times it's just fatherly intuition." He drummed his fingers on the steering wheel.

"So, why were they after me?" I asked after a moment of silence.

"Like I said, psychic blood is rare these days. It's passed down only from mother to child and is very unpredictable."

"From the mother's side," I mumbled, then gasped. "That means, my birth mother must have been psychic too?"

Suppressed feelings began to bubble inside of me. I had never cared too much about knowing my birth parents. I knew that Juan and Maria Hernandez were my true parents. They were the one who raised me and loved me. I had rarely even wondered about what life might have been like if I hadn't been put up for adoption. Now, the feeling was fresh in my mind. Had my mother known I had powers when she left me?

Mr. Dolinsky nodded. His voice brought me back to reality. "Yes, but since you were adopted, we have no idea who that was. Strangely, your birth records are incomplete or lost. That's why it took a few days to get you access to the academy."

"Academy?" I asked. I remembered during the fight the man shouting *"academy scum"*. I had no idea what it meant.

"Just south of here, there's a training academy for psychics. Obviously top secret," He explained. "There's others like it in New York State, California, and New Mexico. This way, we can ensure that any new psychic is able to be given proper training and support."

"Because without it they go Rogue?" I asked.

Mr. Dolinsky nodded. His expression was grim. "Yes. Could you imagine what would have happened if no one had told you about your powers? Every time you got emotional things would break or move? No doubt you'd go searching for answers. We need to catch young people before the go looking in the wrong places and end up hurting themselves or others."

I looked out the window, watching the other cars on the freeway speed by. He was right. I couldn't bear to think of how terrified I'd be if he hadn't saved me. I could barely grasp what was happening now.

We drove for a while longer before turning off into an industrial park. Giant factories lined both sides of the road.

"Where are we going exactly?" I asked, craning my neck to get a better view of the dilapidated warehouses.

"The training academy is hidden here," Mr. Dolinsky explained.

WARNING: DO NOT ENTER. A sign flashed by the window. *RESTRICTED AREA. NO*

VISITORS. CAMERAS PROHIBITED. The signs lined the narrow gravel road.

We stopped at a bridge. The green paint was peeling from the metal. Ahead of us, I could see a small island where the ground was black with soot and iron. The factory sprawled across the landscape. Loose metal creaked and banged in the wind. I could see a large tanker ship docked in the distance. There was no one in sight.

"This looks abandoned." I whispered. How could there be a school here?

"Exactly the point." Mr. Dolinsky said. He rolled down the window and the smell of rust filled the car. He swiped a key card at the gate. There was a whirring sound, and the gate rose up for us to pass through.

We crossed the bridge and the low hum rolled in my belly. It was stronger than it had been before. I wasn't even sure if it was coming from me that time. My body tingled as the feeling expanded through every nerve. I felt nauseous.

"Almost there," Mr. Dolinsky said as if he could sense my discomfort.

We passed over the bridge and onto the island. There was a flash of light and the abandoned buildings disappeared.

A gasp escaped me as I took in the new surroundings.

There were several large buildings. They were modern with hard angular lines made of glass and metal. We stopped in a parking lot which had only a few vehicles. Looming in front of us was the largest building; it looked curiously like a blend of an arena and a school, with the same modern materials as the smaller buildings.

I licked my lips nervously.

"Welcome to the Psychic Training Academy," Mr. Dolinsky said.

I let out a shaking breath.

"Oh, one thing before you go," Mr. Dolinsky added. "No phones or cameras are allowed."

I grimaced. I hated not having my phone. I wasn't addicted to it (I swear!), but the thought of going in there with no way to contact the outside world made my stomach turn. "Alright," I sighed and threw my iPhone in the glove box.

"I'll keep it safe." Mr. Dolinsky promised. He threw his own phone on the dashboard and unlocked the doors.

I got out of the car and closed the door quietly. I didn't miss the dozens of cameras that had been tracking our every move. A drone buzzed overhead. Security was tight.

An American flag was flying high on the flagpole with a smaller flag I didn't recognize flapping below. The sign at the door read: *Federal Psychic Training Academy - North Campus.* When I turned around to look for the bridge, it was gone. I could see nothing past the boundaries of the island.

"How did you do that?" I wondered aloud.

Mr. Dolinsky heard and answered. "Cloaking technology. Not magic," He added with a chuckle. "Just simple force fields and projections."

Didn't seem so simple to me, but I shrugged it off and added it to the growing list of things that I didn't fully understand.

The front door opened, and two people walked out. One was an older man dressed in a navy suit. The other was a tall thin woman dressed in black. Her hair was pulled back in a tight bun and her makeup was as severe as the rest of her features.

Mr. Dolinsky stood at attention. "Major Griffiths. Ms. Blackwell," He addressed each of them with a nod.

"Inspector Dolinsky," Major Griffiths said. He gestured towards me. "I presume this is the new recruit you were telling me about?"

Mr. Dolinsky nodded. "Yes, sir."

The woman was silent; she stared at me intensely.

"Hello," I said. I sounded more confident than I felt. "I'm Bianca Hernandez."

The old man smiled. "It is wonderful to meet you, Miss Hernandez. Such an intriguing young talent we have on our hands!" He motioned towards the school. "Come, let us show you around."

I took a step forward and then looked back at Mr. Dolinsky.

The Inspector smiled. "Go ahead. I'll be here at two o'clock to pick you up. I am not permitted inside the school. Top secret," He added.

I was nervous to go in on my own. I looked from him to the front door and swallowed hard. I summoned my strength and joined the Major and Ms. Blackwell at the entrance. It took everything I had not to look back as the door closed behind me.

Inside the building, nothing seemed out of the ordinary. The front doors lead into a reception area. There was a woman sitting at a desk with a headset on. She was typing away at her computer. There were doors to either side of us and a long hallway with more closed doors. The air was crisp and cool. Ms. Blackwell's heels clicked on the marble floor as we walked down the hall. Everything was so quiet.

Major Griffiths stopped at a door that read *OFFICE*.

"I'll leave you and Ms. Blackwell to take the tour. I still have a few things to finish up regarding your enrollment." He withdrew to his office before I could ask a single question.

Ms. Blackwell walked with her hands clasped behind her back. She had an air of regal beauty and power around her. Her posture was perfect, and every footstep fell into rhythm. I felt like a child compared to her. I bumbled along as she gave me a brief tour of the halls.

All the rooms seemed like ordinary classrooms with desks and computers. Everything was so quiet. It was eerie.

"Excuse me," I said finally. "Where is everyone?"

Ms. Blackwell seemed to be of average height, but her patent leather stiletto heels made her tower over me. "They are in the training labs. That's where our students spend most of their time after they've learned to control their powers better."

I felt heat rise in my cheeks. Was that a dig at me? How much did everyone know about my recent blunders? "Oh, I see," I said and turned my head away to hide my embarrassment.

Ms. Blackwell led me outside to a large courtyard. There was a shady garden and benches along the path for people to sit and relax. The building's tall glass windows surrounded the courtyard. The far side of the courtyard led to another section of the building with a high vaulted ceiling like a gymnasium.

"Are those the training labs?" I asked, glancing at the double doors.

Ms. Blackwell nodded. "One of them." She gestured for me to open the door. "Please, go ahead and take a look."

I opened the door and a wave of humidity hit me. Fans were blowing full force to offset the heat. Mats, ropes and punching bags littered the training room. The collapsible walls were pulled into section off this portion of the room from the others. I could hear people sparing beyond the greenish-gray accordion dividers that went from the ceiling to the floor.

In the center of the room, two boys were fighting. I recognized them immediately as the two who saved me in the park. They were too consumed in their sparring match to notice the door clang shut behind me.

The dark-skinned boy hovered in the air and vanished. As if anticipating this, the pale one turned around and kicked him as he reappeared behind him. They both shouted as they fought one another. Neither of them was holding back.

Ms. Blackwell clapped her hands once to get their attention.

Both boys stopped mid action and turned on their heels to face her. They were both breathing hard and sweating through their t-shirts. Their hands were wrapped for protection. They both looked at me dead in the eye and I felt a shiver run through my body.

Did she know they were the ones who saved me? Is that why she brought me here? How embarrassing.

"Bianca," Ms. Blackwell spoke clearly as she gestured to the two young men. "I'm pleased to introduce you to two of the Academy's finest students: Luke Herrington and Ryland Williams."

CHAPTER SEVEN

The dark-skinned boy gave me a brilliant smile. He was tall and lean with honey brown eyes and hair that was cut short to his scalp. There was an intricate line shaved around both temples that faded to his hairline. "Hey, I'm Luke. Nice to see you again." His hands were wrapped in blue bandages that matched his t-shirt and shorts. He wiped the sweat from his brow on his shirt, lifting the hem just enough to see a quick flash of defined abs.

I looked away. He definitely remembered saving my ass in the park. How embarrassing.

"I didn't think I'd be lucky enough to see you again." The blond guy said. "I'm Ryland." He had a hint of a west-coast accent. His fair hair was nearly as light as his skin and his blue eyes were like ice. He was also fit; he was slightly taller than Luke and dressed completely in black. He wore compression leggings and no shoes.

My eyes met his and the twinge of energy returned. A shrill buzzing sound filled my brain for a moment and stopped when Ryland looked away. Whatever strange connection had been created was silenced.

Ms. Blackwell cleared her throat to get our attention. "Miss Bianca is considering enrolling in the academy. Her powers just emerged a few days ago. I was taking her on a tour of the facilities."

I smiled awkwardly. I felt like a science project or a pet. I had never in my life been the "new kid". I had gone from the same preschool to elementary to junior high and all the way to my impending graduation with the same circle of friends. This was a very new and very weird feeling, especially when I was being looked down at by two incredibly attractive and powerful psychic guys.

I tried to speak, but Ms. Blackwell cut me off.

"Why don't you give our guest a show?" She said. "She seems most interested in training and honing her abilities."

I went redder and looked at the floor. Why didn't she just make me a sign that read I DON'T KNOW HOW TO CONTROL THE POWERS THAT I HAVE EVEN THOUGH I DIDN'T KNOW PSYCHICS EXISTED UNTIL A FEW DAYS AGO!

"Cool," Luke said. "What can you do, anyway?"

I shrugged. "Not really sure yet," I admitted.

"I can read minds, among other things," Ryland said with pride. He grinned as my eyes met his. "It allows me to anticipate my opponents' moves and dominate hand-to-hand combat."

"Telepathy," Ms. Blackwell added. "We use scientific names here."

Ryland shrugged.

"I can teleport," Luke said as if it were no big deal. "I'm also working on apportation."

I blinked. "What's apportation?"

"May I?" Luke held out his hand and Ms. Blackwell handed him a pen from her pocket. He twirled it around in his fingers for a moment and then it disappeared.

I gasped. "Where did it go?"

Ms. Blackwell cleared her throat and raised her hand. It had returned to her palm in the blink of an eye. "As I said, Luke and Ryland are some of our best students. It is not incredible power that makes students excel here; it is the willingness to learn." She gestured to the two guys. "Let's show Bianca what our students are capable of."

They nodded and returned to the sparring mat.

Luke held up his wrapped hands and took on a fighting stance. Ryland stood relaxed with his hands at his sides.

Luke shouted and lunged at Ryland. A split second before Luke reached his opponent, he disappeared. Ryland laughed and turned, his fist lashing out and meeting Luke's shoulder as he reappeared behind him.

Luke caught himself and crouched down, kicking out at Ryland's legs. Ryland fell onto the mat hard and growled; he wasn't down for long.

Luke lunged left and right to avoid Ryland's punches.

I held my breath as I watched them spar. Luke vanished in and out of range and Ryland almost always anticipated where he would re-emerge. They moved in a violent dance that neither of them wanted to lose. Their eyes were locked onto each other's and their muscles were coiled tight. I didn't know anything about martial arts, but in my humble opinion, they were both *freaking awesome*.

Ryland lashed out and Luke went down hard. He lay still on the mat for a moment, his chest heaving up and down as he caught his breath.

Ryland smirked as he stood over his partner. "You're out."

"Not yet," Luke laughed and vanished.

"Shit!" Ryland whirled around but Luke was nowhere to be seen.

Suddenly Luke came from above him, tackling Ryland into the ground and twisting his arm backwards.

Ryland gritted his teeth before begrudgingly tapping out.

Ms. Blackwell clapped. "Well done boys, both of you. I'd say that there are no finer fighters in our entire school."

Ryland and Luke stood and bowed their heads to one another.

"Good game," Luke slapped Ryland on the shoulder. "No hard feelings, bro."

"Right." Ryland agreed, but something dark flickered behind his blue eyes. "One day, I'll beat you, Luke."

Luke threw back his head and laughed. "One day? Maybe. If you keep practicing."

Ryland held up his fists. "I'm ready when you are."

Luke grinned, but the sparring match was cut off by a buzzer. The shrill sound echoed throughout the gymnasium.

I looked at Ms. Blackwell for an explanation.

"Ah, lunchtime," She said.

I swallowed hard. If they used a sound that ear-piercing for lunch, what did they use for an emergency? Not that I wanted to find out. "Lunch? It's only eleven o'clock." I glanced at the digital clock above the door.

Luke laughed. "Eleven is a good time when you start training at six A.M."

I held back a grimace. I was not an early bird. The very thought of waking up before the sun rose made me reconsider even thinking about enrolling.

Ms. Blackwell's eyes lit up. "I have an idea. Luke and Ryland, why don't you take Bianca to the dining hall for lunch? It would be good for her to see what student life is like here at the Psychic Academy. I will rejoin you in about an hour."

Luke and Ryland looked me up and down before agreeing.

"Excellent," Ms. Blackwell said. "Don't be shy Bianca. Soon enough, the academy will feel like a second home." She vanished.

I gasped and stepped back. "What the-"

Luke chuckled. "How did that surprise you? I've been doing it since we met."

I blushed. "Not that. Just wasn't expecting it."

How many times could I embarrass myself in front of these guys before the end of the day? It was so uncharacteristic of me. I was never a bumbling idiot; now I felt like someone who didn't belong here. New girl syndrome hit hard.

"Ms. Blackwell is the professor of psychokinesis and advanced teleportation." Ryland said. His eyes narrowed. "I'm guessing your abilities have something to do with telekinesis, that's why she was assigned to give you the tour. Am I right?"

"I honestly don't know what I can do," I stammered. His gaze made my body prickle with heat. Was he reading my mind right now? How could I tell?

"Come on, man, give her a break." Luke slapped his partner's shoulder. "Bianca, just give us a second to shower and then we'll show you the dining hall."

8

I waited in the courtyard outside. I sat down on a bench, happy to escape the sweaty humidity of the training lab. I caught glimpses of students in the halls through the windows. They traveled in small groups. It looked way less crowded in here than my high school where I had to elbow my way through to my locker on a daily basis.

I glanced up at the sky through the canopy of trees. The sky was a brilliant blue, almost too blue. The force field that surrounded the academy shielded us from unwanted eyes, but I wondered what else it did.

"Nice day, huh?"

I looked over to see Luke. He had changed into form-fitting shirt and pants. His biceps stretched the black cotton t-shirt.

Luke stood at the bench, looking down at me and then to the sky. "The force field always seems to magnify the weather. Don't worry, you'll get used to it."

"That's what everyone keeps saying," I sighed. When I stood, my eyes were level with Luke's jawline. He smelled like mint and soap. I saw myself reflected in his honey brown eyes and looked away.

"I mean it," Luke replied with a smile. "You will. Everyone does. That's why the Psychic Training Academy exists, to help us." Positivity radiated from him.

We locked eyes again. My skin felt hot when I was near him. I wanted to be closer. He seemed like such a nice, sincere guy. Guys as sexy as him didn't normally even look at girls like me. They were the type to chase cheerleaders and beat up nerds. Luke seemed refreshingly down to earth.

Luke leaned in towards me a fraction, giving into the magnetic pull between us.

Was he going to kiss me? Butterflies erupted in my stomach. Then a pulse of energy filled my head. I gasped and pulled away. It went as quickly as it came.

"Ready to go?" Ryland joined us. He was dressed in the same utilitarian black clothes as Luke. His blond hair was still wet, slicked back against his skull. His icy eyes slid from Luke to me.

I shrank away from his cold gaze. "Yeah, I'm starving," I lied.

The pulsing feeling in my head returned and Ryland scoffed. "Alright, let's go."

My mouth went dry. Did he just read my mind? I felt violated. Without a word, I followed them inside the academy.

The halls were empty, and the dining hall was full. With a quick glance I estimated that there were about a hundred or so students ranging from fifteen to twenty years old. Most of them looked to be about my age, but I was never great at judging that sort of stuff. I'd be the world's worst police witness. The dining hall was large enough that not everyone had to sit crammed together, but the clique groups were clearly defined.

I followed the boys to the side of the room where a buffet of food was laid out. It all looked incredible: hot soup, pasta, roast chicken, salad, sandwiches, sautéed vegetables; it was infinitely better than what the cafeteria at my school served, which was why I always let my mother pack a lunch for me.

I suddenly felt very hungry. I waited patiently while Luke and Ryland filled up their plates before fixing a more modest plate for myself.

"There isn't a lot of students at the Academy, it is way smaller than your average high school," Luke explained as we walked back to the rows of tables.

I didn't miss everyone's eyes on me. The typical curiosity of the "new girl"; I did my best to ignore it.

"That's because psychic powers are rare and, unfortunately, dying out." Luke continued.

"Dying out?" I repeated as I sat. Luke sat beside me and Ryland sat across from me.

Luke dug into his pasta immediately. I recognized the ravenous feeling. It was the same after my two encounters with my own powers. Maybe using psychic energy made everyone tired and hungry.

"Yeah, psychics are a rare breed," Ryland spoke up. "We like up less than one percent of the population. What's worse, is that the psychic gene is recessive and only passed from mother to child. In this day and age, psychics breeding with non-psychics is common, and it's watering down our population."

Luke grimaced. "Dude! When you say it like that..."

"It's true." Ryland cut him off.

I looked around at the people surrounding me. Now that Ryland mentioned it, I noticed that there were more male students than female. Everyone was dressed in black, but it could still make out the normal high school type groups: a pack of beefy gym rats, the artsy goth kids, blond preps, awkward nerds, this school had it all. If I didn't know any better, I'd think they were normal kids.

Almost everyone had gone back to eating and chatting. Only a few people glanced my way. I looked down at my turkey sandwich.

"What's wrong?" Luke asked.

"I've just lost my appetite," I replied.

Luke shot Ryland a glare. "Hey, it wasn't about what he said was it? Do you come from a mixed family? I do too."

Ryland made a sound at the back of his throat and shook his head.

"I honestly don't know," I admitted and looked up at each of them. Luke was so warm and comforting while Ryland was so edgy and mysterious. They were such opposites, but I couldn't help being attracted to both of them.

"I was adopted," I said with a shrug. How many times had I told this story to people? It never used to hurt, but now it left so many questions flying around my head. Was my mother psychic? Were they both psychic? Did they know I had powers? Why would they abandon me if psychic children were so rare? Why didn't they want me?

Ryland's icy expression remained unmoved by my story.

"So, you don't know?" Luke seemed surprised. "No wonder you can't control your powers. Uh, no offense," He added with a laugh.

I shrugged and pushed my uneaten sandwich away.

CHAPTER EIGHT

The buzzer rang out to mark the end of lunch. The students filed out slowly towards their next class.

"Ah, I got to get to class," Luke said with a sigh. "I have intermediate teleportation, and if I'm late again, the prof is going to literally kill me." He stood up and gave me an apologetic look.

"It's ok, I'll make sure she gets back to the office," Ryland said.

Luke nodded. "Nice meeting you, Bianca. I hope that I see you again soon." He vanished.

I held back a gasp. It would take me a while to get used to that.

Ryland stood and stretched. His muscles strained against his tight black shirt. "Well, let's get going then. I take it they already showed you the classrooms?"

I nodded. "Just the ordinary ones."

"Yeah, the special training areas are dangerous if you don't know what you're doing."

His words bit at me, but I didn't let it show. I stood up and shrugged my shoulders back. "Can you take me to the office then? I'm sure Ms. Blackwell is waiting for me. And I don't want you to be late for class either."

Ryland shrugged. "I don't care about class. All I care about is training."

I didn't know how to respond to that, so I followed him silently out of the cafeteria and down the hall. The sound of his boots hitting the marble floor echoed around us. I hated the awkward silence.

"So, when did you enroll here?" I asked.

Ryland looked over his shoulder and paused so I could catch up. "I just transferred here in February from California," He said. "My family lives out there. I came here for a different challenge."

I nodded.

"Unlike you and most of the students here, my parents raised me knowing I was psychic. I never went to a normal school," Ryland explained.

I wasn't sure if there was an insult hidden in his words, but I let it go.

Ryland shoved his hands in his pockets. "Psychic powers are normally revealed after puberty." He looked at me and a shiver shot through my body. "But in my case, my family is well known and very powerful."

I nodded again.

"The Williams family is one of the purest families left." Ryland said.

Maybe it was because he never went to a public school or maybe he was just obvious to the cringe-worthiness of the word "pure" when it came to bloodlines. I shook the awkwardness away. "I hope that I'll find out about my family," I said.

Ryland shrugged. We stopped at the office.

I was stuck between the wall and his hard body. I looked up to meet his gaze. "Thanks for walking me back to the office," I said.

Ryland leaned down until our lips were almost touching. "You're very powerful. I know you can't control it yet, but I can sense it." He planted his arms on either side of me and edged closer. "I find it hard to believe that someone as gifted as you had no idea they were psychic. I can't wait to see what kind of chaos you unleash. This semester might just get interesting after all."

I swallowed hard. What could I say? He was so close that I could feel the heat of his body. I wanted to run. I wanted to kiss him. I wanted to escape. I wanted to stay here locked between the brick wall and his body. My heart was pounding in my chest.

Ryland leaned in and our lips almost touched. Suddenly he pulled away at the sound of the office door opening.

"Ah, Ryland," Ms. Blackwell said. "Thank you for walking Miss Hernandez back to the office."

Ryland stood at attention. "Not a problem," He said. "I'll be going to class now." His eyes met mine. "And I'm sure I'll be seeing you again, Bianca."

Why did his icy blue eyes always give me a chill? I nodded like an idiot. "Yeah, ok." My mouth was dry.

Ryland turned and left without a glance back.

"The Major has your enrollment papers ready." Ms. Blackwell gestured towards the office.

Oh crap, I forgot they wanted me to make a decision today. Sure, the school was great, the guys were hot, and the teachers seemed nice enough, but was I ready to enroll?

I followed Ms. Blackwell inside the office. She led me past the secretary who shot me a warm smile and into Major Griffiths' office.

While the rest of the building was cold, spartan and angular, the Major's office was warm and inviting. The floor was covered in thick plush carpet that was the same green as the walls. The furniture was made of mahogany wood. Two chairs were empty in front of his large desk. The Major sat muttering to himself and looking at a computer.

"Ah, welcome, Miss Hernandez," he said as he looked up. "Apologies I was trying to pull up some documents, but the computer seems to be on the fritz. Psychic interference!" He laughed. "You never know when the equipment might go haywire around here." He gestured for me to have a seat.

I sat down across from him. Ms. Blackwell remained standing by the door. Didn't those heels ever hurt her feet? I'd be grateful for the opportunity to sit if I was wearing those. If there was some psychic immunity to foot pain, sign me up.

"So, Miss Hernandez what did you think of the academy?" Major Griffiths asked.

"It was very impressive," I said. That was no lie. I had never seen anything like it.

The Major smiled. "Excellent. Now, I know everything is very new for you, but rest assured you are not the first to show up at our door not knowing a thing about their powers. In fact, it's quite normal. The Federal Psychic Training Academy is designed for exactly that. We're here to help you discover your powers and give you a purpose."

A purpose? Had I not been whining about having no direction only days ago. Everyone else seemed to have it all figured out, while I had no idea what I was going to do. The academy might be my way out of that.

"But what about school?" I realized out loud. "I still have a few more weeks left and exams."

The Major raised his bushy eyebrows. "We can take care of that. It's more important that you're here where you can be safe."

I bristled. "No, I want to finish high school with my friends." I said. I had gone through every year of school with Daniel and Jessica by my side and I would not give that up for anything.

Major Griffiths paused. He crossed his arms and leaned back in his velvet chair. "You do realize that remaining in the general population without being about control your powers is dangerous to yourself and everyone around you?"

I swallowed hard. I hadn't thought of that. "Sir, I only have outbursts when I'm emotional. If I can stay calm, everything will be ok. It's just two weeks," I added.

The Major looked past me to Ms. Blackwell. They exchanged an unreadable glance. He stopped to think. "Well, it's been done before in extreme circumstances," He said. "I suppose we could give it a try. You need to be aware that this is a huge risk, Miss Hernandez."

I nodded.

"I will need to assign someone to keep an eye on you as well. Inspector Dolinsky has been doing a splendid job so far. I'm very thankful that he found you before..." He trailed off.

"Before what?" I asked.

The Major shook his head. "Never mind," He said with a smile. "It's nothing."

If life had taught me anything, it was that when people said it's nothing it was definitely something. I let it go. I had nothing to bargain with anyways.

The Major slid a package of papers across the desk to me. "Seeing how you're eighteen, we don't need your parents' permission. Which, in this case, is incredibly convenient. We try to reduce the knowledge of psychics to the general public as much as possible."

"Wait! You mean I can't tell my parents?" I blurted.

The Major shook his head. "Absolutely not. It is not in their best interest. If people knew about psychics, well, there would be panic and jealousy. Everything the government does is to keep you safe. Our powers are great, but we are vastly outnumbered."

I nodded. He was right. I saw my powers with my own eyes and had been in denial. It was scary when I really thought about it. My parents would have understood, I was sure, but maybe now wasn't the best time to spring that revelation on them.

"You are a unique case. Most times, at least one parent is psychic, and the academy can intervene without a hitch. In your case, being adopted, it complicates things. So, I insist that you do not mention it to your guardians."

"My parents. Maria and Juan Hernandez raised me as their own. I will never think of them as anything less than my mom and dad." I said firmly. I turned my attention to the paperwork in front of me.

While I filled out the information, the Major explained some things.

"For the next two weeks I will organize for you to come and work in the training labs under the care of Ms. Blackwell. You can come after school and train for a few hours. It's better than nothing. Once you graduate, you can begin full time. We have dormitories for students."

I looked up, nearly dropping my pen. "Dorms? But I live so close."

The Major shook his head. "Constant vehicles going in and out of the force field are not recommended. All our students stay on site except on weekends for security purposes. While you are attending part time, I will ask Inspector Dolinsky to chauffeur you." He smiled. "We have our ways, Miss Hernandez. I will ensure that your guardians... parents," He corrected before continuing. "Are not suspicious."

I let out a breath and returned to the tedious forms.

Known allergies? None.
Known medical conditions? None.
Family history of psychic abilities? Unknown.

My hand was cramping by the time I finished the forms. I shook my wrist to get the blood flowing again. "Alright, done."

Ms. Blackwell stepped in and whisked away the documents. "Very good, Bianca. I look forward to beginning your training tomorrow." She didn't smile or sound excited, but I figured that was just thanks to her tight-laced personality.

Major Griffiths was practically beaming. "I'm so glad you've decided to join us here at the academy."

I forced a smile and shoved down my nerves. "I am too." I wasn't sure if my words were entirely truthful. I had too many questions left unanswered. Too "many what ifs" and "whys?". Only time would tell if this really was the best decision for me.

∞

I met Daniel as soon as I got back that afternoon. His father had done his best to reassure me that I had made the right choice, but I was still on edge. Having my best friend by my side was instantly calming.

"So, a boarding school for psychics, huh? That's awesome." Daniel said with a grin.

I waved my hand and looked around the diner. "Shh, keep your voice down. You're the only one who's allowed to know about this. I can't even tell Jessica," I said. I had barely taken a bite of my mac and cheese; my stomach was tied in nervous knots.

Daniel's expression sobered, and he nodded. "Well, it's still cool." He plucked a fry from his plate. "It's going to be intense doing both though. Why didn't you just let them take you out of classes? I mean, there's only two weeks left anyway."

I shook my head. "No. It's a matter of pride. I want to graduate the same as everyone else. No matter what."

Daniel chuckled. "I suppose I can agree with that." He waved another fry at me before popping it into his mouth. "But I want to know everything and if there's anything I can do to help you with exams or whatever. Just say the word."

I smiled. He was always putting everyone else's needs before his own. "Actually, there is something you can do," I said and lowered my voice. "My powers are unpredictable, and I still don't have any answers. They only seem to activate when I'm stressed or upset, so if you wouldn't mind keeping me grounded, that would be a big help."

"Don't I do that already?" Daniel grinned.

"True," I said. "But this time it's life or death."

Daniel grinned wider. "I wouldn't have it any other way." He nudged my bowl towards me. "Now eat."

CHAPTER NINE

I cut out of my last class early so I could meet Mr. Dolinsky and get a ride to the academy.

I told my mom I was studying with my friends. It hurt so much to lie, but the Major was right. I knew my mother better than anyone and I'd bet that if I told her I was off to train in a government facility for people with psychic powers, she'd probably call the doctor and the priest.

Mr. Dolinsky dropped me off at the door with a smile. "I'll pick you up at seven," He said.

I nodded and shouldered my backpack. At least I had Mr. Dolinsky and Daniel to help me through this mess. They were like my second family. "Thanks," I said and waved as he drove away.

The car vanished in a ripple of light as it crossed the barrier. All this technology and magic was going to take a lot to get used to. Sure, they said everything was rooted deeply in science, but it felt kind of magical to me at least.

"Good afternoon, Bianca."

Ms. Blackwell met me in the lobby. She had her hands clasped behind her back. Her posture was flawless as usual.

"Hello," I said meekly.

She turned on her stiletto heel without another word, leading me down the hallway.

The classrooms had groups of students in them. It seemed that nothing remarkable was happening inside when I glanced in the windows. They just looked like typical, bored students.

I followed Ms. Blackwell through the courtyard and into the large training facility. It was empty. The greenish accordion walls had been pushed aside, revealing how large it was; it must have been four times the size of the gymnasium at my high school.

Storage cubes lined the wall by the door. Ms. Blackwell opened the one closest to the door and pulled out a set of black gym clothes. "Here, change into these." She gestured to the change rooms adjacent to us. "We don't need your street clothes getting scuffed up."

I swallowed hard. What exactly were we going to be doing on the first day that might ruin jeans? I decided not to ask and went to change instead.

The locker room was immaculate with bright lighting, gleaming floors, modern benches, and chrome lockers. It took my breath away. Before changing, I checked to see if the showers were equally as impressive, which they were. I was already looking forward to a hot shower in the marble stalls.

I shook myself to focus on the task at hand. I hadn't brought anything with me, so there was no need for a lock. I made a mental note to get one next time anyway. I changed out of my jeans and t-shirt and into the black leggings and tank top that had been provided. I tied my sneakers back on tightly and looked at myself in the full-length mirror. It was the kind of mirror that would be great for taking selfies with, if I was allowed my phone, that is.

I mentally cursed myself for not remembering to bring a hair elastic. My long black hair hung down past my shoulders. I just knew it was going to be a nuisance during whatever physical drills that Ms. Blackwell had planned for me.

I took a long drink from the water fountain before returning to the training room. I was surprised to see that one of the accordion walls was shut to close off our space to a more reasonable square footage.

Ms. Blackwell was standing at the center of the room. She raised her hands in the air and suddenly gym equipment that was stacked against the wall rose up and arranged itself on the floor. Mats, weights, balance balls, and countless other things that I didn't know the names of moved with a flick of her wrist.

"Wow, that's amazing," I said.

Ms. Blackwell looked over her shoulder at me and the corners of her mouth turned up ever so slightly. That was the most emotion I had seen in her so far. "Thank you," She said. "With a little work and a lot of practice, one day I'm sure that telekinesis will be as second nature to you as it is to me."

I felt the glow of admiration in my chest. "I hope so."

Ms. Blackwell's hands fell to her sides, and she turned to face me. Her indifferent expression had slid back into place. "Then, let's begin."

I stepped onto the mat, instantly feeling very nervous. I let out a long breath, letting my hands dangle at my sides. I still had no idea how to summon any powers without being an emotional wreck.

Ms. Blackwell waved her hand and a small rubber ball rose from the ground. It turned around and moved up and down before returning to the mat. She motioned for me to follow suit. "Go ahead, try to move the ball."

I braced myself and held out my hand. I focused on the red rubber ball, just like I had done in the park with Daniel. I waited for the hum of energy, but none came. I sighed, shook out the tension in my shoulder and tried again. Nothing happened.

I groaned in frustration.

"Try again," Ms. Blackwell said, not put off by my failure. "Using telekinesis is like exercising a muscle. It takes practice."

I focused harder, reaching out to the ball and imagining picking it up. After a moment, I swore I saw it twitch just a fraction. My heart leaped up with hope. Almost there. I gritted my teeth and pushed my will towards the rubber ball.

The ball bounced up about a foot.

"Yes!" I shouted and the ball shot up into the air, bouncing off the ceiling and nearly hitting me in the head.

Ms. Blackwell caught the ball in midair. She sighed. "While you're learning, I'd advise you to keep control of your emotions. You never know how objects might react. Telekinesis is an art."

I blinked. Was that why she seemed so void of emotion all the time?

"Again."

I nodded and focused my energy on the rubber ball. I used all my might to ignore everything else around me and try to lift the ball up from the mat. My fingers twitched as I pushed my energy towards the ball. The low hum filled my ears and the ball shot up to eye level. It hovered there for a moment.

I felt my control start to slip. I gritted my teeth and fought to keep my emotions in check.

A bead of sweat trickled down the back of my neck. The tension cut and the ball fell to the ground.

I clenched my fist in frustration. "Why is this so hard?"

Ms. Blackwell shook her head. "Be patient. You just discovered your powers a week ago. There is no shame in slow progress."

I sighed and wiped the sweat from my neck. My arms were getting weak.

Ms. Blackwell clasped her hands behind her back. She was like a merciless drill sergeant. "Again."

"Give me a sec, please." I breathed.

"No." Her voice was icy. "You need to learn how to control your powers or else you will be a danger to everyone around you. If you insist on living outside of the academy, we need to be sure that you won't accidental hurt anyone."

I threw up my arms in frustration. "I'm not trying to hurt anyone!" I snapped.

Suddenly, the balls and weights rose into the air and shot out in a sunburst around me and slammed into the walls.

Ms. Blackwell held up a hand, and the projectiles missed her entirely. If she hadn't blocked them, a ten-pound weight would have hit her right in the face. It fell with a thud at her feet.

My blood went cold. "Sorry." My voice was tiny.

Ms. Blackwell ignored my apology, staying focused on the task at hand. "*Again.*"

∞

When dinner time rolled around, I breathed a thankful prayer. Even after a hot shower, my body was aching and exhausted. My head was pounding. I had never been hungrier before in my life. Now I knew why Ryland and Luke had taken such massive portions at lunch.

I dragged myself to the cafeteria which was not nearly as full as it was last time I was there. It seemed there was no predetermined dinner time; most classes ended at four o'clock, so students wandered in whenever they wanted.

I glanced around but didn't see anyone I knew. These private classes with Ms. Blackwell would only make my isolation worse. If I wanted to break out of the "new girl" label, I would need to make some friends fast.

After filling my plate with roasted chicken, salad, and potatoes, I lost my nerve to introduce myself and sat down alone. No one looked my way. I felt completely invisible.

A quick scan of the cafeteria allowed me to count less than half of the fifty students that were supposedly enrolled. This made the room seem huge, as it could easily seat one hundred people. A small group of jock-type guys were near the wall being loud and obnoxious. Not far from them was a pair of girls who had changed from their black utilitarian clothing into pink dresses.

I looked down at my food and noticed a black mark on the white table. I ran my finger up and down it. It looked like it had been scorched by fire. I shook my curiosity away and ate, mindlessly fading in and out of thoughts. I really wished I could have my phone now; although, like Major Griffiths said, electronics seemed to be unpredictable around psychic energy.

I looked up when I heard someone's heavy boots stop beside me. An African American girl about my age looked down at me. Her dreadlocks were red and black and bundled in a messy bun on top of her head. She wore horn-rimmed glasses and her eyes were dark brown. She had high cheekbones and full lips. She was, in a word, beautiful. Beautiful and intimidating.

I knew that look. "Oh, sorry, is this your seat?"

"Technically, no." She said.

I attempted to get up anyway, but she waved me back down.

"It's a free country. You can sit there." The girl said dismissively and sat down in front of me. She had a plate of vegan enchiladas.

"Alright." I didn't argue. I pushed my uneaten potatoes around on my plate before getting the nerve to speak again. "I'm Bianca Hernandez."

The girl raised her perfectly micro-bladed eyebrows.

I knew that look; I got it all the time. Thankfully, she spared me the usual comment of "you don't look Latino?!" and I didn't have to explain my life's story.

"Phylicia Booker," She said with a smile. "Nice to meet you." She paused to take a sip of water. "I don't think I've seen you around here before. You must be the new girl?"

I nodded. "Yeah, so it seems." I laughed. She made me feel comfortable. Her voice was kind and warm; it didn't at all match her outward tough-girl appearance. She was fit and muscular, but not in a bulky way and, if I had to guess, she was probably almost six feet tall. She looked like a professional athlete.

Phylicia's smile widened. "Ah, I know that look. Not settling in as well as you thought? Don't worry! It happens to the best of us. Especially if you don't exactly fit in with their standards."

"Standards?"

The girl lifted a finger and a small burst of fire appeared. She waved her hand, and the flame vanished in a puff of white smoke and heat.

"Whoa, that's amazing!" I gasped.

"I'm glad you think so," Phylicia said. "I'm the only one on this campus that's pyrokinetic. It's a rare talent that just so happens to run in my family." She shrugged as if being able to produce a flame out of midair was no big deal.

"Everything is amazing to me here." I admitted.

Phylicia nodded. "I heard rumors that you were raised without a psychic parent."

"News sure travels fast around here," I muttered.

Phylicia laughed and her gold earrings jingled. "Ain't that the truth!"

I looked up just as a man walked into the cafeteria. He looked to be in his late-thirties and the kind of guy I'd break my "*I'm not really into older men*" rule for in a heartbeat. His black hair was swept back, showing just hints of gray at his temples. His beard was cut short and neat. He was tall with broad shoulders and his well-tailored suit only emphasized his fit physique.

Phylicia noticed my jaw go slack and looked in his direction. "Ah, that's Professor Turner." She said with a smile. "He's one sexy dude. But don't bother. Even though you're legal, he's not that kind of teacher."

I feigned shock. "I wasn't thinking like that." I could feel the heat rising in my cheeks and it wasn't from Phylicia's fire abilities.

Phylicia raised her eyebrows. "Honey, I know that look. It's hot enough to almost start a fire, but not quite." She winked at me and drummed her fingers on the table.

I watched a flame bounce across her knuckles before vanishing in a puff of smoke. When I looked back up to catch another scintillating glance at Professor Sexy — I mean Professor Turner, he was gone.

∞

I held out my hands and exhaled. With a twitch of my fingers, the five-pound weights rose from the ground and slid onto the shelves effortlessly with a thunk.

"Excellent work, Bianca." Ms. Blackwell said.

A few days of grueling training had brought me surprisingly quick results. I was far from perfect, but at least I could move small items on demand now. I could control my emotional responses. Bursts of anger, frustration, or fear seemed to be the ones that were most likely to trigger a "psychic spasm" as I had come to label it.

We both looked to the door as it creaked open. Luke was standing there in black gym clothes. "Ah, sorry, I hadn't realized this room was being used."

Ms. Blackwell waved her hand dismissively. "It's fine Mr. Herrington," She said. "We were just about to take a break." She excused herself from the room.

I plunked down on a bench and took a drink of water. Using my powers drained me, but it wasn't as bad as it was before training. At least I didn't faint from moving these small objects around.

Luke stopped halfway between me and the accordion wall. "So, how's training?" He asked.

I shrugged. "Tough," I admitted. "But worth it."

Luke nodded. "Ms. Blackwell will run you ragged, but, believe me, she's the best professor this academy has."

I nodded and glanced at the clock. It was past five. "I know it's none of my business, but what are you doing here after hours?"

Luke laughed. "I come to do extra training," He said with a shrug. "My last class is so boring. I come here to burn off energy."

"I barely have enough energy to walk after a training session," I admitted.

"Same. Let me tell you one thing: it never gets easier. You just get better." Luke flashed me a brilliant smile and I melted a little inside. He sat down beside me on the bench.

I hadn't realized I was staring at him like an idiot until he spoke again to break the silence.

"Come to think of it I haven't seen you in any lectures." He tipped his head to the side.

It was then that I realized how close he was to me. I shook myself out of the trance but didn't move away. His warmth was comforting.

"Yeah, I've been working with Ms. Blackwell to get a hold of my powers. Once I graduate high school, I'll be here full time," I said. It didn't even sound real when I said it.

Less than two weeks left of school and then I'd be here training with the rest of them.

"How are your telekinetic skills coming along?" He asked.

I shrugged. "Ok, I guess. There's a steep learning curve."

Luke laughed out loud. "You're telling me! When my powers first manifested, I'd disappear randomly whenever I got nervous. The first time it was just from my house to my neighbor's yard. But the second time, I popped right out of a classroom in my high school and ended up on top of a building downtown. That's when I got help."

I sucked in a breath. "That must have been terrifying."

Luke shrugged. "It was at the time, but now I just laugh about it," He said. "Pretty much everyone has a funny story about their first time."

I smiled and looked at my shoes. Luke made me feel so comfortable. He was sweet, funny, and good-looking. His honey brown eyes lit up whenever he laughed. The positive vibes that radiated from him were almost addictive. I wanted to kiss him.

The door opened and cut off my thoughts. To my surprise, it wasn't Ms. Blackwell, it was Ryland.

"Ah, Luke, I was hoping you'd be here. Up for a little bit of sparring?" Ryland asked. He was also dressed in gym clothes.

Luke tensed up beside me and jumped off the bench. "Always."

Ryland glanced at me. "Ms. Blackwell is in the hall talking to Professor Turner, in case you were wondering."

I had forgotten about my training. "Oh, right, thanks?" I said awkwardly. His icy blue eyes made me forget my words. "Well, I guess I should leave you guys to it."

"Wait," Luke said. "I was just going to ask if you wanted to show me some of your moves, before we got interrupted."

Ryland scoffed.

"Uh, I'd better not," I said meekly. I wasn't sure enough of my control over my powers to let anyone near me but my teacher. The last thing I needed was to accidentally knock someone out with a weight or worse.

Luke looked at me. "Don't let him get to you. Just 'cause he has a pedigree, he thinks he has more talent than the rest of us."

Ryland closed the distance between us. "Say that again," He growled.

The tension was thick, and a low rumble filled the air. I put myself between them, looking up at each of them in turn. "Listen, please don't fight. I'm going to take it easy for the rest of the night, so I don't burn out."

Ryland's eyes met mind. "Fine. Rain check? I'll spar with you tomorrow."

I opened my mouth to respond and then remembered that I had already made plans. "Actually, I won't be here tomorrow. It's prom."

"Prom?" They both repeated incredulously.

"Yeah?" I shrugged. I turned my head back and forth, noticing how surprised they both looked. "What? You do know what prom is, right?"

Ryland rolled his eyes. "Of course, we do!"

"It's just that," Luke added in a gentler voice. "That guy who attacked you last week is still at large. Are you sure you should be out at night?"

My mouth went dry. That guy. The psychic with destructive powers that created earthquakes. The one who tried to kidnap me. "Oh. I had no idea," I said. "I thought it was taken care of. No one's said anything."

"Probably because you've been chauffeured everywhere by that FBI guy." Ryland said.

I didn't bother correcting him. Ryland didn't seem like the kind of guy who would care about people's names.

"Did you tell Ms. Blackwell?" Luke asked.

"I wasn't going to ask permission. It's my life!"

Luke grimaced. "As true as that is, they won't want you risking your or anyone else's safety. Can you imagine what would happen in that guy showed up?"

I didn't want to imagine. I shuddered. "Alright, then what do I do?"

"Don't go." Ryland said. His tone was flat and unsympathetic.

I seethed. "No, I want to go! I need to. I've been looking forward to it all year." My voice nearly cracked. I had compromised almost everything to be at this academy, but I wouldn't give up the most important night of high school. "Besides, I already bought my dress."

Ryland rolled his eyes.

"Well, there is one way," Luke said after a moment of thought. "If we have added security, I'm sure everyone would agree to it. You just need to bring one of us as a date."

CHAPTER TEN

In the end, I chose to go with Luke. His temperament was better suited to a long evening of small talk. Besides, I really wanted to sneak that kiss I'd been craving. Ryland was coming along too in order to keep an eye on the perimeter. They really took missions seriously for guys who were just students. No wonder they were both top of the class.

"Mi niña hermosa," My mother said with tears glinting in her eyes.

I felt beautiful in my dress. It was made of purple silk that clung to my body in all the right places and fanned out in a mermaid hemline. My strapless push-up bra helped add a little bit of cleavage. My shoes were strappy, silver, and the heel was about half an inch higher than I was comfortable walking in. But if I could survive three-hour training sessions with Ms.

Blackwell, I could survive one night with sore feet — it'd be worth it.

I smoothed the fabric over my hips and turned around to catch a glimpse in the mirror. For one night, I hoped I could just forget all this craziness that had happened over the past week and be a normal eighteen-year-old again.

My mom snapped a few pictures with her phone.

There was a knock at the door.

I grabbed my clutch purse and kissed my mom on the cheek. "Love you. See you tonight."

"I'll be waiting up for you," My mother said with a smile. "Now, go have a good time."

When I opened the door and saw Daniel, I couldn't help but notice how handsome he looked in his black suit and tie. He waved to my mom as I shut the door behind me.

"You look beautiful, Bianca," He said.

"Thanks," I said shyly. Where had this man come from? It was as if he replaced the boy I grew up with overnight. Daniel had been a bit of a late bloomer, but I finally was able to see how handsome he was.

Daniel motioned to the driveway where his father was waiting in the car. "Shall we?"

I nodded. "Actually, just one thing," I said.

"What is it?" Daniel's eyebrows drew together with concern.

"Well, I know that we said we were going together as friends," I said. "But, because of what's being going on with *the-you-know-what*,

I had to have a bodyguard come with me and pose as a date."

Daniel's eyes widened with realization and then an indifferent mask fell over his face. "Oh," He said with a nervous laugh. He held up a white box with a corsage that matched my dress. "I see. Well, I can't say I'm not disappointed."

My heart strained when I heard the hurt in his voice.

"But it's ok. I understand." Daniel took the corsage out of the box and tied it around my wrist. "Your safety matters more to me than anything."

"Thank you," I said and kissed his cheek. "You're a good friend."

Daniel nodded slowly and then cleared his throat. "Anyway, let's get going." His shining confidence that appeared when I first opened the door had faded.

Guilt took its hold on me and I felt suffocated. What else could I say? I had been looking forward to prom as much as he had. Wasn't it better that I was here instead of being cooped up at home or at the academy for my own safety or the safety of others? It seemed that the professors were much more concerned about the wellbeing of the community more than my own health. Whatever their reasoning, I was thankful that Luke had convinced them everything would be alright as long as I had some trained psychics to intercept anything that tried to ruin the night.

"You look beautiful," Mr. Dolinsky said as I gathered the hem of my dress so it wouldn't get caught in the car door. His smile faltered when he sensed that the silence between his son and I was more than typical teenage nerves. "What's wrong you two?"

Daniel shrugged.

"The academy has put security in place for tonight," I explained. "One of the top students is going to pose as my date. He's meeting us there." I shifted uncomfortably as Mr. Dolinsky's eyes shot from me to Daniel. "It's for the best." I added.

Daniel agreed half-heartedly.

Mr. Dolinsky frowned. "I see," He said. "Well, if there is any psychic disturbance, make sure you call me right away. It would probably have been smarter to have actual agents around instead of students. But I suppose a student would blend in better." He shrugged and pulled out of the driveway.

I nodded.

We drove in silence until we reached the banquet hall. Limos and minivans were lined up as parents dropped of their kids. I could hear the music from outside. Strobe lights flickered; balloons and glittering streamers decorated the entrance in a blue and gold arch.

I was beyond relieved when I got out of the car and the fresh air hit me.

Daniel's door slammed with an ounce of excess force and his dad drove away.

I looked to Daniel and forced a smile. "Hey, I'm really sorry about this. But, let's try to have a good time, ok?"

Daniel nodded. "Yeah. Like I said, your safety is more important to me than anything."

We caught a glimpse of Jessica and her girlfriend Mia. They were almost at the doors. Jessica waved at us to hurry.

I waved back, but she had already disappeared in the crowd of students.

Daniel looked around. Dinner would start soon. "So, where is he?"

I looked over my shoulder and as if by magic, Luke appeared.

Daniel hissed in surprise and took a step back.

"Luke!" I gasped. "You shouldn't just teleport in and out like that!" I kept my voice low. It didn't seem that anyone around us noticed.

Luke grinned and shrugged his shoulders. He was dressed in a dark navy suit with an orange pocket square and tie that complimented his dark complexion. His hair was freshly cut with a neat lineup that went straight across his forehead. "I think I know what I'm doing."

"Where's Ryland?" I asked.

Luke tipped his head in the direction of the parking lot. "Nearby. Keeping an eye on everything. He may be a jerk sometimes, but he's great at what he does. With both of us around, you have no need to worry."

Daniel kicked at the ground, reminding me he was there.

"Oh, sorry!" I stepped back to introduce them. "Luke, this is my best friend Daniel. His father works for the FBI. Daniel, this is Luke. He's going to be our added security tonight."

The boys shook hands. Luke was friendly and warm, but Daniel was on edge. "Pleasure," He said. He straightened his jacket "We'd better get inside before they serve dinner."

"Oh, one more thing." Luke said. He revealed an orange corsage that matched his tie. "For my date." He tied it around my wrist above the one Daniel had given me. "I never got to go to my prom because of training. I figured I'd may as well do it right."

Daniel scoffed and began up the stairs to the entrance.

I shot Luke a glance and followed Daniel.

Luke linked our arms together as we walked. "Did I do something wrong?" He whispered.

"No," I said. "But Daniel and I promised we'd go together and now this has really thrown everything off."

"Is he your boyfriend?" Luke asked.

"No, but he's my best friend and I don't think he was counting on a third wheel. No offense."

Luke shrugged. "I'm here to keep you safe. If he was really your friend, he'd understand."

8

The tension between Daniel and Luke tainted dinner. I tried my best to ignore it. Introducing Luke to people I knew as my boyfriend who went to college out of state. No one asked follow-up questions, which was a blessing.

The ballroom was decorated with the same school colors as the entrance. The prom committee sure had done a great job. I wasn't normally into this kind of stuff, but I couldn't help but be impressed.

We sat a round table with Jessica and Mia. Jessica was in a red mini dress while Mia, who generally preferred the androgynous look, was rocking a white tuxedo. I saw between Daniel and Luke to prevent any conflict that might be caused by the palpable discomfort.

The center of the room was being cleared away for dancing and the DJ turned up the volume. Now the real party could get started. I was thankful that the first hour had gone off without a hitch.

"I can't believe you didn't tell me you started seeing someone," Jessica whined as she finished her second plate of dessert.

I shrugged and glanced at Luke. "We just met, actually."

Jessica clasped her hands together. "That's so cute."

Mia shook her head and laughed. "Jess, you're such a hopeless romantic."

Jessica feigned shock. "Well, doesn't everyone need a little but of romance in this world we live in? Love is what makes it all worthwhile." She kissed her girlfriend's cheek. "Still, you should have told me right away!" She scowled in my direction.

I didn't miss the hurt in Jessica's voice. It was her personality to keep everything light and bubbly, but she wasn't happy with me. I wasn't surprised. She was my go-to friend for anything boy related. I couldn't tell her anything that was honest about Luke.

Jessica and Mia went off to the dance floor, leaving us in silence.

I sighed and looked down at my hands. Having two corsages on my wrist was just a reminder of the two worlds that I now had to play a part in. How was I going to handle this?

As if reading my mind, Daniel leaned in. "This is just the start. This is what happened to my parents. Once you're psychic, there's a part of your life that you need to hide from other people. It destroys relationships."

I swallowed hard, tears prickling at the corner of my eyes. He was right. I couldn't bear the thought of losing one of my best friends because I had to hide half of my life. I stood up and brushed some crumbs off my dress. "I'm going to go to the washroom. I'll be right back."

Daniel called after me, but I ignored him.

I kept the tears at bay until I left the ballroom. My vision blurred as I went looking for a washroom to hold my private pity party in. I didn't need to ruin anyone else's night. I found the washroom and it was empty. I locked the door behind me and hunched over the sink, crying big, ugly, mascara-stained tears.

There was a pop of pressure in the room and when I glanced up at the mirror, I saw Luke standing behind me.

"Luke!" I gasped and turned around.

Luke handed me a wad of tissue to clean up my face. "Don't cry. Please," He said. "It's never a good look when a girl cries all her makeup off."

I wiped my eyes and a tiny laugh escaped me. "Thanks, Luke."

He tipped his head to the side as he looked at me. "I heard what your friend said and maybe it didn't work out for his folks, but my parents are still together. My dad didn't find out about psychics until I started at the academy. If a marriage is on the rocks, maybe being psychic is an easy scapegoat; I'm sure that wasn't the only thing."

I shrugged and dabbed my eyes.

"Ryland and I disagree on pretty much everything. But it's probably always easier if two psychic people are together. At least you can rely on each other for support when no one else in the world would believe you even if you told them. We make up around 1% of the population. I won't sugar coat it — it gets lonely."

I looked up at him, feeling a warmth glowing inside me. He was so sweet and so caring. I knew I had made the right choice for him to take me to prom. Even if it was just for security. I smiled. "Thanks, Luke."

"Anytime." Luke smiled.

I let myself fall into his arms. He held me close and we were silent for a moment. I listened to his heart beating slow and steady in his chest. His grip on me was secure and gentle.

I was never one for dating. I had tried a few times, but most guys in my school were complete idiots. I hadn't really counted on meeting anyone worthwhile until college. Standing here felt right. It felt like I imagined it would.

I looked up at him. "Luke?"

"What is it?"

I could see myself reflected in his eyes. Even the harsh fluorescent bathroom lighting and the sound of a leaky tap wasn't enough to ruin this moment. "If things were different and we didn't need security, would you have gone to prom with me anyway?"

To answer my question, Luke leaned down and pressed his lips against mine.

I melted into his kiss. Shivers ran through my body as I wrapped my arms around his shoulders and leaned into him.

Our kiss turned hot almost instantly. I parted my lips and our lips wrestled against one another. I moaned into his mouth as he lifted me up onto the counter, his hands roaming down my back and over my hips.

I ached for more as he pulled away.

"Does that answer your question?" Luke asked with a spark in his eye.

I kissed him again. My body felt as if it were on fire. I wanted more. I wanted all of him. I wanted everything that I had been holding back from my entire life. Our bodies pressed together, and I could feel his hardness against me.

A low rumbling sound interrupted our kisses. I pulled away from him, feeling the countertop shake. The lights were flickering and swaying from the ceiling.

"Earthquake?" I breathed.

Luke's expression darkened. "No. Looks like we have an unexpected guest."

CHAPTER ELEVEN

The ground trembled underneath our feet. The now-familiar hum filled my ears and my stomach lurched. "What is that?"

"If I had to guess, it was probably that guy that attacked you last week in the park." Luke said.

The rumbling patterns were eerily familiar. That night in the park seemed like a lifetime ago now. My fear flooded back, remembering the raw power that guy possessed.

"Alright, let's go handle this." Luke said. He pulled his hands from my waist and loosened his tie.

I followed him out of the bathroom. People were running in all directions, most towards the exit. We fought against the current of people and towards where the pulsing feeling was strongest. I tried to catch a glimpse of Daniel or Jessica in the crowd, but there were too many people.

"Earthquake!" Someone shouted.

Luke pulled me to the wall so we wouldn't get trampled. "Stay close!"

I nodded and held onto the back of his suit jacket. The room was empty when we got there. Tables were overturned, the DJ's set up had crashed to the ground, broken glass littered the floor. It was too quiet.

Just as the ground began to shake again, a man appeared. He floated above us in the center of the room and grinned down at us maniacally. "Ah, so you are here, pretty girl. I knew I could sense your power."

His voice made me want to throw up and the way the floor was swaying certainly didn't help.

Luke stepped in front of me and took up a fighting stance. "You're not getting away this time."

The man scoffed. "Oh, academy scum, don't make me laugh." He had sallow skin and a hooked nose. His hair was dark, and his clothes looked old and dirty. If I didn't know what he was capable of, I would have thought he was just some crazy homeless guy. But I had seen firsthand what kind of psychic power he possessed.

The man raised up his arms and pushed them forwards. Several chairs rose into the air and shot towards us at tremendous speed.

Luke didn't hesitate. He grabbed my hand and teleported.

It happened in a blink. One moment I was standing by the door with chairs barreling towards me, the next I was back out in the hallway. I felt dizzy. I leaned against the wall as my vision blurred in and out of focus.

Luke was panting. He squinted when he looked at me. "Bianca, I need you to stay out of the way."

I gritted my teeth. "No way. I'm going to fight with you. I'm not useless. I have training!"

"Not enough." His voice was firm. "Please, I can't hold him off if I'm worried about protecting you too. It takes twice the amount of energy for me to teleport another person. If I do it too much, I won't have energy to fight."

I opened my mouth to argue, but the shut it with a snap.

Ryland came around the corner with his daggers in hand. "Seems like you two could use some help." He smirked.

I had never been so happy to see him. "That guy from the park is back!" I shrieked.

"I noticed." Ryland gestured to the ballroom where the power was radiating from. "Alright Luke, ready to take this asshole down once and for all?"

Luke nodded. He turned back to me. "Stay here. Promise me."

"Fine," I said. "But don't get hurt."

"We'll do our best. Don't worry your pretty little head." Ryland said and then ran off with Luke to fight.

I sank down on the floor. What use was all this training if I wasn't good enough to help? I could hear sirens approaching. Police and ambulances must have been on their way. Then I remembered Luke's instructions.

I kicked off my strappy shoes and dashed off through the empty hallway. I hiked up my dress with one hand as I ran towards the washroom to find my purse. The ground rumbled beneath my feet.

When I swung the door open, I found three girls hiding. They were shaking and their makeup was smeared. "Get out of here!" I shouted. "Can't you see there's an earthquake?" The lie came out easier than I would have expected.

They screamed and ran out in a flash of multi-colored taffeta and clicking of heels.

My purse was still where I left it beside the sink. I fumbled to find my phone and tapped Mr. Dolinsky's number.

He picked up on the first ring. "Bianca? Are you safe? Daniel just called me. He said something weird is going down."

I could hear the sirens on the other side of the phone. "Yes. There's a psychopath psychic guy in the ballroom. He's destroying everything."

"I'm already on my way. I want you to get out of there." Mr. Dolinsky ordered and then hung up.

I leaned against the counter and let out a shaking breath. The bathroom floor was cold against my throbbing feet. Everything should be fine now. The regular cops were on the way and the FBI. Luke and Ryland could hold him off until then. Right? Somehow, I didn't believe my own reasoning.

Another shake reverberated off the floors and the walls. The lights flickered and then went out with a pop. I was plunged into complete darkness. I took a moment to gather my senses before feeling my way out of the washroom and into the hall which was equally dark. About a moment later, the emergency generator kicked in and dim safety lights glowed above every door.

I followed the dim lights down the hall, keeping one hand on the wall and one clutching the hem of my dress. I laughed at my past self for thinking that prom was going to go off without a hitch. How dare I assume that my new life wouldn't totally ruin this night for everyone? I would have let out a cynical laugh if I hadn't been worried about being heard by that psycho.

The sounds of fighting grew louder and louder with every step. I stopped just outside the door, remembering Luke's instructions. It probably would be the smarter thing to just get the hell out of there and let the professionals do their job. But I couldn't run away now. This was all my fault, and I'd never forgive myself if I didn't help them.

I peeked around the door. The ballroom was in ruins. Tables were broken, chairs strewn all over, glasses and plates shattered against the walls. The weird guy continued to hover in place, using his telekinetic powers to throw cutlery and DJ equipment in all directions.

Luke and Ryland were an incredible team, despite their tense relationship. They moved together in perfect rhythm.

I pulled back out of sight and lifted my hand. I focused on a chair that skidded out into the hallway. My fingers twitched, and I felt the hum vibrating in my body. The chair lifted slowly. I clenched my fist and pushed with all my energy to throw the chair back into the ballroom, aiming directly at the weird guy.

I heard him shout as I hit my mark. I couldn't help but cheer in my head. Maybe I wasn't so bad at this after all.

Just as I lifted my hands to attempt throwing a trash can, a voice entered my head.

"We told you to get the hell out of here! I don't know why, but he wants you. Stay hidden!" It was Ryland's voice in my head.

I cringed and fell back against the wall. How could he do that? It gave me shivers to think that my thoughts weren't private around him.

A shout echoed in the ballroom and I peeked around the corner.

The sleazy guy was down, finally. He held up his hands, but the shattered glass did nothing but tremble. His powers were exhausted.

Luke teleported across the room and appeared at his side. He stomped his shoes down on the man's wrists. "I said, stay down!" He shouted. "You're not getting away this time."

In the park, the man had teleported. His powers must have run dry. He didn't have enough energy to teleport anymore.

Ryland pointed one of his long daggers at the man. "Who are you? What do you want? Who are you working for?"

The man let out a raspy laugh and spat in Ryland's direction. "Go ahead and kill me. I'll never tell you."

My heart froze. Kill? Ryland and Luke couldn't kill him, could they? We were just students.

Ryland let out a low laugh and wiped the spit from his cheek. "Don't tempt me." He brought the dagger closer. "Besides, I don't need you to talk in order to find out what you know." He grinned.

The man's eyes widened in realization and he started shouting nonsense. He sang ABCs, recited the national anthem, anything and everything he could think of to drown out his thoughts and keep Ryland out of his head.

Ryland hissed and kicked the man in the jaw. "Shut up!"

"Ryland, stop!" I shrieked as I ran out of my hiding spot. "Don't kill him!"

All three looked my way. Luke's jaw went slack and Ryland glared. "I told you to get out of here."

"And I want you to get out of my head!" I shot back, clenching my fists and making the shattered glass and tableware clatter against the marble floor.

"Bianca!" Luke shouted. "Get out of here before you get hurt!"

That moment of distraction was all the man needed. With a shout he drew up every last ounce of his energy. His powers ripped the glass from me and shot it in an arch around the room. The tiny shards bit against my skin and tore my dress.

There was a rumble and a pop. The man disappeared. We lost him again.

∞

I sat on the curb with a blanket around my shoulders. Ambulance lights flickered red and blue all around me. Most of the students had escaped without more than a bruise or a scrape. There were a few twisted ankles, but that was the worst of the injuries. Ryland, Luke and I were less lucky. The paramedics cleaned and patched up the dozens of tiny cuts from the glass. Ryland and Luke were pretty banged up from the fight, but nothing serious.

"Bianca!" I looked up to see Daniel. He ran to my side and knelt down. "Are you ok? I was so worried."

I nodded silently and pulled the gray blanket around me tighter. "I'm fine." My voice was small and weak.

Daniel sat down beside me on the curb. Most of the students were gone now. "If it makes you feel any better, no one really knows what happened. They think it was an earthquake or something."

"What do you think?" I asked.

Daniel jerked his head in the direction of two FBI vehicles. "Well, I know better than that, especially when the special units show up." He shrugged. Blue and red washed over us as the last ambulance pulled away.

Across the parking lot, I could see Inspector Dolinsky talking to Ryland and another older man that I didn't recognize. Luke appeared from behind one of the vehicles and sat down on my other side. He had a bandage across one of his cheeks.

"Luke! Are you ok?" I asked.

Luke winced as he stretched out his legs. "I'll be fine." He had lost his suit jacket at some point during the fight. His white shirt was tattered and bloody.

"It's all my fault." I sighed. I was too tired to cry. A headache was pounding in my skull. My mouth tasted like dust and blood.

"It's not your fault." Daniel said. "I shouldn't have said anything about Jessica."

I looked up. "Jessica! Mia! How are they."

"Fine. Mia's dad picked them up when you were in the ambulance getting cleaned up." Daniel said.

I relaxed a fraction. "Oh. Good."

"She was so worried about you being stuck in the building." He added. "Seems she's not as upset with you as I thought."

I shook my head. "I'll make it up to her."

"Daniel!" Mr. Dolinsky's voice carried across the parking lot. He motioned at his son.

Daniel sighed. "I guess I need to get going so I can let you guys do your job." He said and got to his feet. He limped a little when he walked. "I'll catch up with you after, ok?"

I nodded, my heart breaking a little as I watched him walk away to his dad's car. My friends were injured because of me. Luke and Ryland could have been killed because of me. Just because I wanted to go to some silly dance. I choked back a sob.

"Hey," Luke put his hand on my shoulder. "It's going to be ok. In a few days everyone will forget this even happened."

"How did they cover it all up?" I asked.

"Probably the same way they made my classmates forget the day I teleported. I don't know how they do it. But it's a special unit of FBI, right? They can do anything." His expression darkened. "Maybe we don't want to know."

That made me uneasy.

"Honestly, it will probably be easy. Just say someone spiked the punch, things got out of hand, a stampede ensued, and everyone got too wasted to remember. It practically writes itself." Luke sighed.

I looked up at the night sky. A plane was directly above us, the white and red lights flashing in the blackness. My chest ached. I didn't know much about this world, but I did know that there was no way I was going to put my friends at risk ever again. This was my fight, and I had to keep them safe.

Next time that weird scum bag guy came for me, he'd regret it.

CHAPTER TWELVE

I shouted and let the energy flow through my body. "Hyah!" I kicked out.

Luke dodged my foot and took a step back. "Good job!" He laughed.

I stopped to wipe sweat from my forehead and take a gulp of water. Since prom night, I had become refocused on my training. I convinced the Major to let me spar with Luke and Ryland after my sessions with Ms. Blackwell.

Luke closed the gap between us, and my heart fluttered. We hadn't kissed since prom night. I wanted him so bad, but I didn't want to make things weird during training. I felt so torn. My body and my mind were fighting each other, and my heart was caught somewhere in the middle.

The training room door opened and two guys I didn't know walked in. They nodded at Luke and continued past the accordion doors to find their own space. There seemed to be a strange segregation between groups of psychics based on their skills. In the week I had been here full time, I had only spoken to Luke, Phylicia, and Ryland.

Ryland was as cold and indifferent as ever. He was still pissed at me for messing up the fight at prom and letting that guy get away. No matter how many times he swore he wasn't actually going to kill that guy, I didn't believe him. His powers were strange and strong. I still didn't understand everything that he could do, and it didn't look like he was going to reveal his secrets anytime soon.

Luke stretched and threw the quarterstaff he was using down onto the mat. "I think we should take a break, Bianca." He rolled his shoulders and cracked his neck.

I was relieved when he admitted to getting tired. Sparring was very different from using my powers with Ms. Blackwell. This was hand to hand combat, something that I had zero experience in before. Growing up, people assumed because I looked Asian that I could kick their ass with my innate knowledge of martial arts, but I had never even thrown a punch until I started training.

I nodded. "Yeah, sounds good. I'm starving."

8

After a shower, I met up with Phylicia in the cafeteria. She had taken back her usual spot with the singe marks on the table. She had a book in one hand and a sandwich in the other. She looked up with a smile.

"Hey Phylicia," I sat down and set a large portion of pizza and fries down in front of me. I had never eaten so much before in my life. Of course, I had never worked out so much before either.

"What's up girl? You look beat!"

I nodded. I was still waiting on my exam marks from high school. I had been pulling all nighters studying and training. Now that was finally over. Mr. Dolinsky and the Major said they were working through some "confidential details" on their end before I was set up in the dorms, which meant being chauffeured back and forth every day as well.

My parents hadn't asked any questions, so I didn't say anything either. Once all the details were set, I'd be moving in on campus. I was actually looking forward to that now.

"How's training going?" Phylicia asked as she closed her book.

I shrugged. "I think it's going well, honestly. But it's draining me. I'm so tired all the time."

Phylicia made a sound of understanding. "It gets easier."

"That's what everyone's been saying," I laughed.

I felt a prickle on the back of my neck and looked up. Ryland was standing by the door and staring at me. I looked away, but I could still sense his presence. He barely spoke to me outside of training; even training and sparring seemed like a chore to him. Part of me wanted to break down his walls and the other half wanted to flip him the bird.

No one really paid much attention to me at all now that the "new girl" label had worn off. Phylicia swore it was because I spent time with her, and she had been shunned due to her unique powers.

I glanced up again and Ryland was still staring at me. I sighed. "I'll be right back, ok?"

Phylicia's eyes went from me, down the long tables and to the doors where Ryland was standing. "Oh, boy trouble? Be careful with that one, alright?" She warned. "He leaves broken hearts wherever he goes."

I snorted. "Yeah, don't worry about that. We're not exactly on good terms right now. I'm pretty sure he'd rather get me expelled than take me out on a date." I threw my gym bag over my shoulder and walked towards him.

Ryland didn't so much as flinch when I glared at him. "What?" I demanded.

"I needed to talk to you," He said.

"Can't you come sit with me like a normal person?"

Ryland frowned. "I was trying to send you a message. It seems that you can't always hear me."

I growled and stomped out of the cafeteria to avoid making a scene. He followed me. "Can't you stay out of my head?" I shouted.

His cold indifference didn't so much as crack. I knew he had emotions; I had seen them firsthand. Now he was like a blank slate every time we spoke. Was he really still pissed about the prom night incident? How immature. Out of everyone, his injuries were the least serious. Not even a shred of glass had scratched his god-like face.

"Well, that's the problem. I can barely get in," Ryland said.

My mouth fell open. "Do you not get how weird it is for me knowing that you're trying to read my mind all the time. Or how much it freaks me out when I hear your voice in my head. I get that you need to train, but I want you to leave me out of it."

Ryland crossed his arms over his broad chest. His biceps flexed against his tight black shirt. "Fine," He said. "I guess you don't want to hear that the Major finally approved your file and you can move in tomorrow."

I gasped. My anger melted away into a weird ball of excitement and dread. "Tomorrow? What about my parents? How am I going to tell them?"

Ryland rolled his eyes. "Don't you know that the secret service can do pretty much anything they want? I figured you'd at least get that by now."

I had never met someone who irked me as much as him. I bit back the snide remark at the tip of my tongue. "I'm going to see the Major." I pushed past him and made my way down the hall without looking back.

"Enjoy your last night at home," Ryland called after me.

His words set chills down my spine.

∞

It felt so good to go to sleep. I passed out almost immediately after getting home. When I woke up the next morning, I felt refreshed and a lot less tense than I had been after training. It was Saturday, so there was nothing going on at the academy for me. Even psychics took the weekends off.

The Major had explained to me that I'd be moving today. I still had no idea how it was going to happen, but I packed my bag anyway. I didn't need much besides some casual clothes and the usual girly stuff. The academy provided all our training uniforms and our classroom uniforms looked pretty much identical, but with less spandex. Everything was black, cut close to the body and meant for quick movement. Every time I got dressed in my training gear, I felt a tiny bit like a spy from the cheesy comics that Daniel always read when we were in junior high.

I brushed my hair and my teeth, got dressed, and headed downstairs to find something for breakfast, or was it brunch? It was nearly noon, but I could eat eggs and bacon pretty much any time of day.

When I arrived at the foot of the stairs, I heard muffled voices coming from the living room. I hesitated and held my breath, leaning it to listen. Two of the voices were undeniably my parents, and the most baritone one was Daniel's father, Inspector Dolinsky. The fourth voice I did not recognize.

I tiptoed over to the living room and caught a glimpse of my parents talking to Mr. Dolinsky and some other middle-aged woman. She had long blond hair tied into a high ponytail and was dressed entirely in black. I knew from the moment I saw her that she must also be from the academy or the secret division of the FBI. I could sense psychic power radiating from her.

"Yes, you should be very proud of your daughter. She is moving away to an elite college today. It's her dream." The woman spoke slowly and evenly.

When my parents repeated her, I realized what was happening. They were in a trance. They were being hypnotized. I stormed into the living room. "What's—" I stopped mid-sentence. The woman held up her hand and I froze in place. I could not move or talk; I was like a statue in the middle of my own living room.

Mr. Dolinsky looked at me and put a finger to his lips.

I tried with all my might to move, but I was caught in her powers. Anger surged through me. How dare she hypnotize my parents! And Mr. Dolinsky was in on it. I needed answers now. I pushed against her psychic grip, but I was no match for this woman.

She pursed her bright red lips and narrowed her eyes at me. It was a warning, no doubt. She then turned back to my parents and resumed her soft tone. "You are so proud of her. She is going to a school far away, but you can still see her on weekend sometimes."

My mother and father smiled but their eyes were blank and dark.

My heart ached seeing them like this. My parents looked like zombies; their arms hung loose at their sides. My mother was still dressed in her housecoat with her hair wrapped up in a silk scarf. Their unblinking eyes waited for further instructions.

The blond woman sighed and snapped her fingers.

My parent's heads fell limp to their chest as if they were sleepwalking.

The woman turned on her heel to face me fully. She put her hands on her wide hips. "If I let you go, are you going to be quiet?"

I could only blink. I didn't want to be quiet. I wanted to run to my mom and dad and shake them out of that trance. I had no idea what kind of weird psychic brainwashing I had walked into, but it needed to stop.

Mr. Dolinsky came to my side. "Bianca do not panic. No harm has befallen your family." His voice was gentle and sincere. "We just needed to plant a false memory that you had been accepted into a special college program halfway across the state. It won't hurt them. It will allow you to train full time at the academy." He gestured to the woman. "It's ok, you can let her go Agent Thompson."

The woman, also known as Agent Thompson, waved her hand towards me and I was released from the bond.

I stumbled and fell onto my knees. I took a giant breath and blinked my eyes furiously. "You don't have to brainwash them!" I protested. "I don't want to attend the academy if it means lying to more people."

Agent Thompson rolled her emerald green eyes and scoffed.

Inspector Dolinsky crouched down beside me and put a hand on my shoulder. "It's going to be ok, Bianca," He said. "This won't hurt them at all. I thought you were looking forward to joining the school full time?"

I shrugged.

"Miss Bianca," Agent Thompson spoke up so I would look at her. "I promise you that my skills do no short or long-term damage to the minds of people I hypnotize. Sometimes it is necessary to interfere with the thoughts of normal people to prevent them from finding out about us. Imagine how distressed they would be if they found out the truth."

I slammed my fist down onto the carpet. "So now everything I live will be a lie."

Inspector Dolinsky and Agent Thompson were quiet, that was all the confirmation I needed. I struggled to my feet and pulled away. "I hate lying. I don't want my life to be a secret. I didn't sign up for this!"

"Once you've completed training, things will become more normal again." Mr. Dolinsky reasoned.

What was normal anymore? Would I ever truly be normal again? My heart ached with the thought of having to keep secrets from my parents. Would they end up hating me like Mr. Dolinsky's ex-wife? Would they feel abandoned or left out like Jessica and Daniel? I wasn't ready for this decision. Hell, less than a month ago I didn't even know what I wanted to do after graduation, and now it seemed that the world had it all planned out for me whether I liked it or not.

A hot tear trailed down my cheek as memories from prom resurfaced. I had to do whatever it took to keep them safe, even it meant lying to them. Every night I was here, I put my parents at risk. I let out a long shaking breath and set my shoulders. "I understand. I will not let them be hurt by anyone who is after me."

Agent Thompson's eyes met mine and there was a glimmer of understanding beneath her straight face. She nodded and snapped her fingers.

My parents stood back up properly and blinked their eyes a few times.

I stood frozen as their eyes widened and they broke into huge smiles. The memories were false, but the emotions were real.

"Oh, Bianca, we're so proud of you!" My mother said and ran over to hug me. "Such a wonderful opportunity. See, I told you everything would work out."

My father joined us and patted my head like he used to do when I was little. He wasn't much for physical displays of affection. "I know you're on a full scholarship, too. I'm so proud. Let me know if you run into any financial difficulty though, alright?"

I nodded, tears forming at the corners of my eyes. I pulled them both into a group hug and let out a sob. "I love you, Mom and Dad. So, so much. I promise I'll make you proud."

CHAPTER THIRTEEN

My dorm was better than I could have imagined. The interior of the building was just as modern and well kept as the rest of the facility. I hauled my suitcase along beside me through the white halls up to the third floor of the dormitory building.

I found my door, 310, and swiped the key card. The pocket door opened with a hydraulic hiss and the lights flickered on as I set of the automatic sensor. The room was fairly spacious, with a bed in one corner and a desk opposite it. There was a mini fridge, a closet filled with training clothes, a laptop computer, and a huge TV mounted on the wall. The desk had a land line phone for calling anyone on the outside. Cellular devices were prohibited.

The blinds on the small window were shut tight. The air had a hint of lavender scent to it. There was no kitchenette or washroom. I had found the communal washrooms earlier, which were even more luxurious than the ones I used after training.

I closed the door behind me and flung my suitcase of the pristine white bedding.

The floors were coed, but we each had a private room; I was thankful for that. The last thing I wanted was to get partnered with some girl I didn't know who snored or talked in her sleep or something like that. I wondered what sort of psychic things might happen during sleep to someone who levitated or used fire. I'd have to ask Phylicia.

I shrugged off the rambling thoughts and unpacked my suitcase. My casual clothes fit neatly beside my black training gear in the closet. I added my favorite photo of my parents and I from last Christmas on the desk.

I kicked off my sneakers and collapsed down on the soft bed. I stared up at the ceiling and let out a long sigh. I wanted to call my parents, but how could I keep up this lie that Agent Thompson had buried into their subconscious. The guilt made my stomach cramp up. Daniel's words flowed through my mind again and I shook them away.

Just as I found myself beginning to nod off, there was a knock at my door. I sprang from my bed and pressed the button on the wall. The door slid open and Phylicia appeared.

"Ah ha, so you did move in!" She said. She was dressed casually in sweatpants and a distressed t-shirt that looked so effortlessly chic; they must have been designer. "Why are you here moping in your room? Let me take you on a tour!"

"That would be great," I said. Anything to get me out of my own head and socializing would be beyond therapeutic at this point.

I slid my shoes back on, checked my hair in the mirror, and then followed Phylicia out.

"The dorm is five floors, everyone has private rooms, there're washrooms and showers on every floor and co-ed lounges on floors five, three, and one. There's also a twenty-four-hour gym in the basement." Phylicia rattled off the stats as we walked down the hall. In another life, she would have been an excellent real estate agent.

At the end of the hall just past the elevators there was a huge lounge. The doors were open and opposite wall was lined with floor-to-ceiling windows to let in the June sunlight. Couches, chairs, and tables were nestled in groups. There was a giant television, gaming consoles, and a library of books, DVDS, and board games on the far wall.

My breath caught in my throat. "Wow," I said.

The room was almost empty. A girl I recognized from the cafeteria was sitting curled up in a chair reading a book. She was dressed in over-sized black sweater and black tights. She wasn't wearing shoes. She was one of the girls who hung out with the "goth-kids" as I had labeled them.

"Where is everyone?" I asked Phylicia. There were over one hundred students that attended the academy, but this place seemed like a ghost town.

"It's Sunday, most people go home on the weekend. To be honest, I like the quiet." She kept walking towards an alcove filled with snack machines.

"You don't go home?"

Phylicia flinched. I immediately regretted what I said. She shook her head. "No, my parents are too busy for me. They're entrepreneurs who only know how to show their love with money. Besides, I'm eighteen. I'm no baby."

That explained her expensive wardrobe. "Oh, I'm sorry," I said.

Phylicia shrugged it off. "Whatever." Her face brightened a moment later. "Hey, wanna go see what's on for lunch? I'm starving."

"I could eat," I agreed and made a mental note not to bring up her family life again.

∞

I couldn't sleep.

The rest of the day was pretty uneventful, even as the other students came back. The cafeteria was packed at dinner time. The lounge of my floor was busy too. I glanced in on my way by, but the tiny goth girl wasn't there. Phylicia had a room on the fourth floor; 412. I could get down there directly using the stairwell at the end of the hall. I couldn't help but wonder which floor Ryland and Luke were on.

I tossed and turned for three hours before giving up on sleep. I threw on some of my training clothes, laced up my sneakers tight and stuffed my key card in my bra. Maybe if I went to the gym and ran on the treadmill for a while, it would tire me out enough to grab a few hours of sleep before dawn.

The halls were dark and empty. Most people retreated to bed before ten o'clock, knowing they'd have to be up before sunrise. I took the stairs quickly and quietly to avoid anyone else who might be up and who might try to stop me from going to the gym at one in the morning.

I swiped my card to open the door. The gym was huge. There was a weight area, countless cardio machines, and a large open floor with yoga mats stacked near the side. It was completely empty. The windows that faced the halls were mirrored for privacy so only someone inside could see out.

Relieved to find the gym empty, I picked a treadmill and random, plopped a bottle of water into the holder and turned it on. The pace increased slowly, and I had only been on for a few minutes when I heard the door open.

"I didn't think I'd be seeing you here." Ryland said.

I pushed the *STOP* button on the treadmill and whirled around. "What are you doing here?" I tried to suppress my breathing. I hadn't exactly been one for jogging or working out before coming to the academy. To be brutally honest, my cardiovascular skills were pretty much nonexistent.

"I'm assuming the same thing you are." Ryland shrugged. He waved me away. "Anyway, do your thing. Don't bother me."

I scowled at the back of his head as he walked to the weights section of the gym. What a jerk.

I started up the treadmill again but couldn't get back to the pace I was running before being interrupted. I wasn't sure if it was because my legs were tired or if it was because the treadmill, I had chosen had a perfectly unobstructed view of the free weights area where Ryland was doing pull-ups.

Ryland's white tank top and gray sweatpants left nothing to the imagination. He was like a Greek god. He made each pull up look effortless, then as if to spite my amazement, started doing them one handed. His muscles flexed and released in a steady rhythm.

I forced myself to look at the screen in front of me that was counting down how many minutes I had left to finish the mile. Ten minutes and I could leave. I wasn't about to go early just because his chiseled muscles were enough to make me drool. A girl had to have some dignity.

I pushed a button to increase the speed just a touch. As soon as this mile was done, I'd leave, I promised myself.

When I dared to glance up, Ryland had moved from the pull-up bar and was stretching. I groaned inwardly, unable to take my eyes away. From what he lacked in kindness and emotional intelligence, he sure made up for in pure animal attraction.

Ryland's eyes met mine in the mirror and I looked away.

"Shit," I whispered. My face was hot and red. I kept my eyes fixed dead ahead of me until the timer chimed. The treadmill slowed to a stop, and I hopped off. The cool water relived the raw feeling in my throat. My legs were shaking.

"Leaving so soon?" Ryland called to me from across the gym.

I ignored him, grabbed a paper towel to wipe off my machine.

"Hey, don't ignore me." Ryland was suddenly at my side. His white tank top clung to his chest.

I sighed and tossed the paper towel into the garbage. "What is it?"

"You don't have to leave just cause I'm here." Ryland said.

I blinked. Was he trying to be nice?

"I mean, I know I'm distracting, but I can't help it."

I frowned. If he was trying to be nice, he just ruined it. What a typical boy. I shook my head. "No, I just needed to burn off some energy. I'm going to bed."

As I turned, Ryland grabbed my wrist and pulled me towards him. "Can't sleep?"

I tensed for a brief second and then felt my strength melt away when I looked into his icy blue eyes. He was such an asshole. Such a sexy, ripped, beautiful jerk. I was powerless when our eyes met. I couldn't even be angry at him anymore. My voice faltered as I tried to find an excuse.

"Don't leave," Ryland said. "Catching up on some training would be good for both of us."

I swallowed hard. Why was my mouth so dry? Why did I want him so bad? Before I could talk myself out of it, I leaned forward and kissed him.

Ryland groaned against my mouth, pulling me towards him and enclosing his arms around me.

I shouldn't be doing this. I knew better than this. But it the moment I didn't care. I just wanted to feel him against me and his hands running through my hair. This was so wrong. What if we got caught? The worries flickered and faded away as his tongue pushed against mind.

I whimpered. My nerves felt if they were on fire and his strong hands moved down to my waist. "We shouldn't do this," I whispered against his mouth.

Ryland pulled away as I looked into his eyes. "We should. There's nothing wrong with what we're feeling. I want you, Bianca."

The icy blue of his eyes was utterly hypnotizing. I ignored the deep hum that was vibrating around us and kissed him again. It was electric; was it the power of two psychics coming together that was creating these waves of energy?

"I want you too," I whispered as he trailed kissed down my neck. Shivers ran through my body.

"Come up to my room." He demanded. Ryland's voice was low and growly.

I snapped my eyes open and froze. That was too much too soon. I gently pulled out of his grasp. "No, I can't." I shook my head.

Ryland grabbed my hand so I couldn't back away. "I know you want to."

A burst of energy exploded in my head. I shrieked and wrestled out of his grip. "Hold up, are you trying to get into my head?"

Ryland looked offended. "No! Why would I do that? I don't need to read your mind to figure out that look in your eyes. Bianca, I want you. I'm not playing games. I swear."

How could I trust someone who could read my mind? The hot desire that was burning inside of me abruptly went cold. "Sorry, I just," I fumbled over my words. "I can't do this right now."

"Bianca, wait!" Ryland called after me as I ran out the gym. He didn't follow me, but for some reason I wished that he had.

CHAPTER FOURTEEN

I was not a morning person.

My alarm went off at five o'clock in the morning. I don't think I had ever been awake before sunrise before in my entire life. I was exhausted. It didn't help that I had only managed to get a few hours worth of sleep.

I dragged myself to the communal showers, got cleaned up and dressed, and then stumbled out of the dormitories to the main building.

Ryland wasn't in the cafeteria. I couldn't decide if I was relieved or upset at this realization.

The first drop of coffee that hit my tongue gave me new life. I ate an omelet and toast for breakfast, alone as usual. Today was my first "real" day of classes. Mentally rehearsed my schedule: first class was *Ethics of Psychic*

Talents, second class was *Telekinetic Theory and Methods*, and after lunch I had a solid four-hour block of physical training. For the first time since grade school, I was actually excited to get to class.

The ethics class was in a standard lecture room. I was early, so early in fact that the teacher hadn't even arrived. I picked a seat all the way at the back to avoid any "let's quiz the new girl" or stares from my other classmates. I flung my notebook and pencil case down on the table and leaned my forehead on my arms. Six a.m. classes might just be the death of me.

Slowly, other students began to pile in. The lecture room had about forty tiered seats; I looked up to watch them silently as the students filed in and found their seats. I knew Phylicia wasn't in this class, so I wondered if anyone else I knew would be.

Ryland? I shoved down the fiery hot thoughts that accompanied his name. Why was someone who was so sexy such a jerkface? I mean, I knew the answer, but it didn't stop be from being disappointed. Why couldn't there be a guy with well-defined abs *and* a good personality? Was that too much to ask?

"Hey Bianca."

Speak of the devil.

I looked up at the familiar voice. *Luke.* I smiled. We hadn't had any time on the sparring mat since the incident at prom, so I hadn't been able to see him. "Hey, I didn't think I'd see you here. This is a first-year course."

Luke shrugged. "There wasn't room on my schedule last year. Besides, don't get too caught up on first year versus second-year stuff. People enroll at all sorts of different ages, depending on when their powers show up. The classroom training isn't exactly linear." He ticked his chin at the seat beside me. "Can I join you?"

"Sure!" I scrambled to pile up the pens that had rolled out of my pencil case, so he'd have space. There was a moment of silence and then I spoke. "Actually, I think I've learned more about psychics outside the classroom so far."

Luke nodded. "Yeah these classes are just for the theoretical stuff. Take notes but don't take it to heart. Everything changes when you're in the real world."

Remember what I was saying about abs and a good personality? Luke had it; the unearthly angelic glow around Ryland just made me forget it sometimes. Luke made me feel warm and happy. He never made me think I was stupid or weak.

I realized I was staring at him and quickly looked away to hide my red cheeks.

The teacher walked in and my jaw fell to the floor. It was the one and only *Professor Sexy*, also known as Professor Turner. He wore a navy blue suit with no tie. His hair and beard were smooth and flawless.

I sat up a little straighter as he pulled down the white boards to prep for the lecture.

Maybe this class wasn't going to be so bad after all.

Luke nudged my hand with his. "Hey, Bianca," He said.

The warmth of his touch snapped me out of my daydreams. "Yeah?"

"I was wondering," Luke's eyes locked onto mine. His nice guy temperament never watered down is confidence. "Do you maybe want to do something tonight? After dinner?"

His words caught me by surprise. *Like a date?* My stupid mouth betrayed my brain. "You mean, like a date?"

Luke smiled. "I'm ok calling it that if you are."

The feeling of butterflies erupted in my stomach.

"Alright class, let's get to work," Professor Turner said as he twirled a dry-erase marker between his fingers. His eyes drifted around the classroom until they fell on me. "Ah, I see we have a new student today, why don't you introduce yourself to the class?"

I groaned inwardly and bit my cheek. So, the sexy teacher had an evil streak. I forced myself to sit up straight. "Uh, hi everyone," I said but only really looked at him. I didn't want to make eye contact with anyone I didn't know. "I'm Bianca. Happy to be here."

"And what is your psychic talent, Bianca?" Professor Turner prompted.

"Telekinetics." I replied. That answer seemed to satisfy his curiosity, so I slouched back down in my seat. Now was a time I wished that I could just teleport out of here.

Luke leaned over and whispered. "So, I'll meet you in the first-floor lounge at seven?"

∞

I arrived at the first-floor lounge right at seven o'clock; I didn't want to be early or seem too eager. I was never really good at navigating this whole dating thing, that's what I needed Jessica for. The realization made my chest ache. I missed my friends.

Luke was already there. He wore distressed jeans and a white v-neck t-shirt. I had never seen him in casual clothes before and I was very impressed. He smiled when he saw me.

I hoped I looked as good as his expression hinted that I did. I hadn't brought too many casual clothes with me, so I chose a pair of dark jeans and an airy baby-doll-style blouse. I smiled back at him shyly.

Luke pushed off the door frame to meet me halfway. "You look beautiful."

"Thank you," I said, relieved. I left my hair down after being unable to get it in an acceptable ponytail. I tucked my long black hair behind my ears. I glanced in the lounge; it was full of students watching a movie or doing their own thing. "So, what did you have planned?"

Luke began to walk. I followed him. "Well, the lounge isn't conducive to a private conversation, so I figured we could go outside. Have you explored the grounds yet?"

I shook my head. "Only where Ms. Blackwell took me on the first day."

"Great," Luke said with a grin. "There's a lot to show you then." He opened the door and the evening air hit us. The sky was painted pink and blue above us; it would be dark in a couple of hours. It smelled sweet, and it felt like freedom.

We were silent for a little while. Luke showed me a walking path near the dorms that led around the larger facility buildings and to a garden. It was like a mini oasis complete with a pond and a small grove of trees. I instantly felt at peace when I saw it.

"It's beautiful," I breathed.

Luke nodded. "I wanted to show it to you. It's my place to escape the stress of training. It's the campus' best kept secret."

A moment of silence stretched between us. It wasn't awkward. It was content. The pond fountain bubbled in the background. We stopped at a bench and sat down.

"Bianca," Luke said and turned to face me. "I just want you to know that I can't stop thinking of prom."

I felt my cheeks getting warm. Was he talking about the kiss or the psychic attack that I screwed up?

"The entire night was wonderful," Luke said as if answering my unvoiced question. "It helped me feel normal, even if it was just for a few hours."

I relaxed and smiled. I couldn't contain my feelings, because he was saying the exact same thing I had been that night. "Me too," I said. "Well, at least until it all went south." I laughed.

Luke chuckled. "Yeah, but I wouldn't trade it for anything. You were stunning. Your friends were nice. It was like I was a normal kid again."

I leaned in and brushed the top of his hand with mine. "I'm guessing you've been training for a while?"

"Since I was sixteen," Luke said. "I've been here for three years honing my skills. Teleportation takes longer to master than most other talents."

"But you're amazing at it. I've seen the speed in which you work when you're training. It's incredible!"

"Incredible for someone who hasn't seen it before." He glanced at me, with a *no offense* expression. "Yeah, I can do short distances better than anyone here, but it's the long distance that takes time to master."

"Long distance?" I repeated.

Luke chuckled. "Yeah, like, if we weren't stuck here in the academy, I could teleport you to Chicago for some real deep-dish pizza in the blink of an eye."

"I'd like that." I admitted. Pizza was my favorite, but everyone liked pizza. I wanted him to whisk me away to a city I had never been to in an instant. The thought was exhilarating.

"Well, if you like pizza, then once I master it, I'll take you to Italy." Luke held my hand.

I leaned in closer to him. "All the way to Italy?"

Luke nodded. "That's what I'm stuck on. Teleportation across large expanses of water is as difficult as it is dangerous."

"So, let's just stick to Chicago for now." I smiled. The pull between us was growing stronger. I wanted him to kiss me like he had at prom: pure unbridled passion. I craved his taste, his smell, and his touch.

Luke wrapped an arm around my shoulder and ran his fingers through my hair.

I eased into the crook of his arm, allowing myself to surrender to his strength. I felt safe and secure, and most of all, comfortable. My heart was pounding but not in the same way that Ryland had made me feel in the gym last night.

Ryland and Luke. They were like two sides of a coin. Light and dark. The sun and the moon, yin and yang. How could I choose between them? I couldn't have it both ways.

I shoved away that thought. It was much too early to be worried about choosing or even anything long term. I had to stay in the moment. I rested my head against his shoulder and let the relaxing sound of the fountain wash over me.

"Bianca, I really like you," Luke said after a minute. "I feel like I can be myself around you."

I looked up, and he kissed me. I leaned forward and found myself in his lap with his arms around me. Reality melted away; all I felt was his touch and his familiar scent of mint. My eyes locked onto his as I forced myself away from the kiss. I drummed my fingers against his wide shoulders. "Luke, that was," I trailed off.

"Amazing?" He finished for me.

I nodded. "I know what you mean when you say that you feel like yourself when we're together. Everyone here seems on edge, like they all have something to prove. But you're so... normal?"

Luke chuckled and kissed me again. "Bianca," He said as broke away from my lips and brushed against my cheeks. "We're not that different. I know what its like to just wake up with powers one day. I'm not from a prestigious home like Ryland. My mother is psychic, but she didn't think I had any powers, so she never told me about it. It was a rude awakening the first day I randomly teleported."

I didn't miss the far off look in his eye, as if he was reliving the memory all over again. It probably haunted his dreams the same way the fire in the museum haunted mine. The confusion. The fear. It wasn't something that could easily be forgotten.

"Luke, I —" I was cut off by the screeching sound of alarms.

Luke jumped to his feet and set me down on the bench with a single fluid motion. He was at attention now; the relaxed boy had vanished.

"What is that?"

Luke held up a finger for me to be silent. After a moment he spoke. "That's the emergency signal at the teleportation point." He motioned towards the direction of the training facility. "Something isn't right. Come on!"

I chased after him as fast as I could. I made a mental note to keep up my treadmill practice so I wouldn't get left behind in the dust once I was cleared for field training. I supposed that I should be grateful he ran instead of teleporting and leaving me all alone in the dark.

I followed Luke to the building. Alarms were blasting at full volume and bright security lights flashed. At the back of the building there was a chain-link fence enclosing a patch of pavement. It didn't quiet match the rest of the landscaping. It stuck out like a sore thumb.

There was a woman laying still on the pavement. I squinted and realized it was Ms. Blackwell in black and gray field training gear. She was face down and I couldn't tell if she was breathing. Her hand was inches away from an emergency button that she must have pressed before passing out.

Luke sucked in a breath and teleported into the enclosed area. Just as he did, two teachers appeared. One I didn't know and the other was Professor Turner. They ran out of the building and threw open the enclosure gate.

"What happened here?" Turner shouted over the alarm as he punched in a code to disarm it.

Luke helped roll Ms. Blackwell over. "I don't know. I was outside on the walking path when I heard the alarms."

The other teacher, who was an older woman with gray hair and a petite frame, examined Ms. Blackwell. "She's unconscious, but other than that she seems fine."

The alarm and flashing lights finally slowed to a stop.

I breathed a sigh of relief. Professor Turner looked directly at me and I straightened up. Was I supposed to be watching this? I felt awkwardly out of place.

"She's in field gear. Where was she assigned? Where is her student?" The other teacher fired off questions at Turner.

Professor Turner shook his head. "Give me a second." He pointed at Luke. "Young man, we don't need your assistance. Take our little spectator home." He gestured in my direction.

Luke nodded and teleported out of the enclosure and to my side. "Come on, Bianca," He said. "Let's go back to the dorms and let the teachers sort this out."

I hesitated, unable to tear my eyes from Ms. Blackwell's limp body. Sure, she worked me like a dog during our training sessions, but I'd never wish any harm on her. What happened? I needed to know. But the expression on Turner's face was enough for me to know that I was not wanted here.

"She'll be fine. Let's go." Without warning, Luke grabbed my hand and teleported us back to the safety of the dormitories.

CHAPTER FIFTEEN

"Attention students. There will be a mandatory assembly today at thirteen hundred hours. Do not be late." A crackling voice echoed through the halls.

I looked up at the speaker and wrinkled my nose. "Thirteen hundred?"

Phylicia laughed. "That means one o'clock in the afternoon. The Major still uses way too much army talk."

"Oh," I said with a sheepish chuckle. I felt dumb for not knowing that. I shrugged it off and drank the last of my water. "I guess I'm going to miss some training." My stomach twisted nervously.

My training was supposed to be with Ms. Blackwell and I hadn't heard a word about her condition all morning. It didn't help that Luke was missing from class first period either. His absence weighed heavily on my mind. I forced myself not to think about it. I was making connections where they were none. Stupid anxious thoughts and nothing more, I reassured myself.

Phylicia glanced at my plate. "You've barely eaten anything, what's up?"

I didn't tell her about what happened last night. I didn't want to accidentally let loose any rumors about Ms. Blackwell. I shrugged. "Homesick."

Phylicia narrowed her eyes. "Are you sure it's not boy trouble?"

I didn't even have to lie this time. "I'm certain it's not boy trouble." I kept my voice as light as possible to elevate her worries; she didn't press further. "Anyway," I said after a moment. "I'm going to get changed for training so I can go directly to the facility after the assembly."

Phylicia nodded.

I hoped that I didn't offend her. I just couldn't say anything until I knew for sure what happened.

I ran into Luke at the cafeteria doors. "Luke!" I exclaimed as I literally ran right into him.

Luke caught me by my arms. "Whoa, slow down, Bianca!" He laughed. "I was just coming to find you."

"Oh? Why?" The feeling of butterflies returned.

"Major Griffiths wants to see you," Luke said. "Well, see *us*, I suppose."

The butterflies curled up and died.

∞

Major Griffiths office was dark and made me feel claustrophobic. I kept my eyes on the carpet as Luke and I waited for him. Luke didn't know what the meeting was about either, which only added to the feeling of dread.

The door opened with a creak and Major Griffiths walked in. Professor Turner followed him.

"I suppose you might know why you've been called in today." The Major said as he sat down. Turner stood behind him with his hands behind his back.

My chest went tight. Was it because Luke and I were out roaming the grounds past dinner? No, that couldn't be it. It had to be about Ms. Blackwell.

"Is Ms. Blackwell alright?" Luke voiced my fears.

The Major nodded slowly. "Injured, but we suspect she will recover."

Luke and I let out a mutual sigh of relief. "Thank goodness."

"But there is a more serious matter at hand. We do not know how she was injured last night." The Major continued. "You two were at the scene first. Do you remember seeing anything suspicious?"

I shook my head and glanced at Luke.

"We didn't," Luke said. "When we arrived, she was alone and unconscious. It would be my guess that she used her last ounce of strength to teleport back to the academy."

Professor Turner frowned. "Why would you think that?"

The Major held up his hand to prevent an argument. "Mr. Herrington is one of our finest students. He works with Ms. Blackwell on advanced teleportation. However, I suppose we will have to suspend that until she is feeling well again."

Luke sank back in his chair. The disappointment on his face was undeniable.

"At the meeting today, we are going to share some of this news with the students. But not all of it," The Major said. "Effective immediately we will not allow any teleportation in or out of the academy without explicit permission from myself. We cannot take any risks." He waited for a nod from Luke before continuing. "Unfortunately, the student who was on fieldwork with Ms. Blackwell has disappeared."

Luke's mouth fell open in shock. "Are they in limbo?" The look on his face was enough to tell me that whatever limbo meant to psychics, it was a very bad thing.

The Major shrugged, which seemed very out of character for him, but he must have been more shaken by the news than either of us. "We don't know. His tracker was disabled. I have informed the authorities. There is nothing else we can do now but wait." He paused. "That's why I need to stress the importance of the teleportation ban. I trust that this information is safe with the both of you."

Luke and I exchanged glances and nodded. "Understood."

The Major let out a long sigh and drummed his fingers on his mahogany desk. "Alright, that's everything then. Oh, actually one more thing," He added as I stood up. "Bianca, can you stay back for a few moments, I wanted to check in to see how your first week was going."

I sat back down and watched Luke leave. He looked over his shoulder before shutting the door. His faced had paled since the Major discussed the teleportation ban.

"What's limbo?" I blurted before Major Griffiths could speak.

The Major shook his head sadly. "It is an awful, awful fate. Sometimes when psychics teleport, they don't have enough energy, or something disrupts them. When that happens, they often disappear. *Forever.* Those who don't have no recollection of what happened between the time they left and the time they returned, which in some cases can be *years.*" He shuddered. "Truly horrifying."

I sank back in the chair. Now I knew why Luke's face had turned to ash; I wouldn't doubt that it was one of his biggest fears.

"Don't let it trouble you," The Major said with a forced smile. "After all, Ms. Blackwell came back, so it is likely her student will show up soon. I have some of the best agents on the case, including Inspector Dolinsky."

That was a relief. I knew Mr. Dolinsky wouldn't rest until the student was found. If he cared as much about the other students as he did about me, that kid was in good hands.

"Now, on to other matters," The Major said. "Seeing how Ms. Blackwell is going to be off for some time, I wanted to introduce you to your new teacher. Jack Turner is one of the finest experts in telekinetics that I know."

I looked up at Professor Turner, who was still standing patiently. He needed no introduction. He was handsome, charming, and caring.

Turner nodded towards me with a slight smile. "Miss Bianca," He said. "I've heard great things about you. I'm very happy to cover for Ms. Blackwell in the interim. I understand that you've been doing private training in order to get you up to speed?"

I nodded. His voice made me want to melt.

"Excellent. I'll meet you in the training facility at three o'clock." Turner said. "I'm sure our time together will be most enlightening."

∞

Why was I fixing my makeup and hair before training?

Everyone else was in silent shock after the assembly while I ran off to the dorms to shower and change. I guess the news didn't hit me so hard because I had already spoke to the Major; I still acted as surprised as I could.

I layered on mascara carefully, using the mirror in my room. I changed into my training clothes and brushed my hair into a sleek ponytail. My heart was fluttering despite me trying to tell myself to calm down and not think of a teacher in a romantic way.

I went to the training facility, not bothering to stop at the cafeteria for a snack. I wanted to be early to warm up so we could get started right at three. I wondered how his training techniques would vary from Ms. Blackwell.

The training facility was busy this time of day. Our closed off space was near the back of the gymnasium-sized rooms. I used the narrow corridor that ran between the accordion walls, which I learned were bulletproof and fireproof to allow many students with a variety of skills to all practice at the same time without having to worry about a stray fireball or something of the sort. They weren't soundproof; it felt like being in the middle of an action movie with a blindfold on. I could hear all sorts of fighting and yelling around me.

When I got to my area, Professor Turner was already there waiting for me. He looked calm and completely at home. He had changed out of his suit into compression leggings and a loose gray t-shirt. Seeing him dressed so casually lit a fire in my chest. For someone who was nearly twice my age, he sure was fit.

"Good afternoon, Professor Turner." I said. It was a miracle I didn't trip over my words.

Turner looked up from his clipboard. "Ah, Bianca," His glowing smile was enough to make my heart flutter. "Please, call me Jack. We don't need any of the formal stuff outside the classroom."

I didn't argue.

"Let's begin." He gestured to my feet. "Go ahead and take off your shoes. Having your feet flat on the floor can help you connect with your powers."

I noticed that he too was barefoot. I kicked off my shoes and socks before beginning my usual warm-up stretches. I took deep breaths, holding my hands over my head and stretching my arms to the sides and forwards and backwards. I arched my back and shook the tension out of my body.

When I glanced up, I noticed that Professor Turner was staring at me. I bolted upright, wishing I had left my hair down to hide how red my face had become. "Sorry, just warming up."

"Not at all," Turner said. "Don't let me stop you. I was just reviewing your progress so far." He tapped the clipboard with his blue pen. "Would you say that your meeting with Ms. Blackwell have been challenging?"

I nodded. "Yes, very much so. I didn't even know I had powers until recently so you could say I've been starting from the ground up."

He nodded in agreement. "And it seems you've built up a good base. But now I think it's time to push you a little further."

I bit down on my cheek. Push me? Was I ready? Ms. Blackwell was still focusing on the basics for me. "I can try," I said after a moment.

"Good," Turner said. "That's the kind of motivation I like to see in my students. Forgive me for saying, Ms. Blackwell is a lovely woman, but she has gone soft in the past few years." He paused. "But I shouldn't gossip with a student. Why do you show me what you can do?"

Knowing what I did about Ms. Blackwell, I couldn't imagine her being any more hardcore than she was now. And he said she went soft? That was more than a little terrifying.

I laid out the usual tools on the mat in front of me. Two weighted balls, a five-pound plate and a ten-pound plate. I remembered vividly when even the five-pound weight seemed impossible. Now it was too easy.

One by one I stood before them, held out my hand and lifted them with my mind. I brought them up to eye level and then back down on the mat.

Turner scribbled some notes on the clipboard. "Bianca, your file says that you've been causing explosions when agitated. Has this happened at all on campus?"

I shook my head. "No. Ms. Blackwell has taught me to control my anxiety. My powers are much more focused now."

Turner made a noise and wrote more notes. "That's what I was worried about." He muttered to himself.

"Worried about what?" I asked.

Turner looked up from his notes and caught me in his alluring eyes. "Well, it's just that, Ms. Blackwell had good intentions, but she might have actually made things harder for you," He said. "Bianca, you are a very powerful psychic. I can feel it when I'm near you. All of this focus is good, but it might have dimmed your shine."

I was shocked. "But before I was destroying everything. That can't be good either."

Turner closed the distance between us, and I held my breath. "Destruction has its purpose in this world. Do not be afraid of being powerful." He kept his eyes on me and held up his hand. With a flick of his wrist, the ten-pound weight rose into the air. The cast iron plate groaned and buckled; a moment later it fell back to the ground in two pieces. He had torn it in half as easily as wet cardboard.

I gasped.

"That is what you will be capable of if you train with me, Bianca." Turner said. "Do you want that kind of power?"

The feeling of his breath on my neck gave me goosebumps. "Yes."

CHAPTER SIXTEEN

The ban on teleportation had a great number of students upset. Those who were used to the freedom were irritable and paced in the halls. Those who normally teleported home on the weekend because their families lived too far away were trapped here with the rest of us.

I sat in the lounge with a book on my lap, but I wasn't reading. I moved my hand over the pages, turning them back and forth with my mind. I couldn't get Professor Turner out of my head.

Phylicia went to bed an hour ago. The group of guys playing Fortnite on the X-Box left shortly after. Now there was no one left in the lounge except for the tiny goth girl. She was tucked away in the corner reading with headphones on. I got the hint and didn't bother talking to her.

I flicked my wrist upwards and made the book levitate above my head.

Turner's words rolled through my mind constantly. Did my training with Ms. Blackwell really dampen my powers? Did I have the potential to do bad ass stuff like rip metal apart? Maybe eventually.

Suddenly, a loud thump rang out through the room. I startled, and the book fell on my head. I flung it off and bolted to my feet to see the goth girl was laying face down on the carpet and convulsing.

I had never seen a seizure before, but I knew enough about first aid to guess this was it. I ran to her side, turning her over gently and making sure that she wouldn't hit her head.

The girl's eyes rolled back in her head and she was drooling. Her body trembled and jerked unnaturally.

I instinctively reached for my iPhone before remembering it wasn't there. "Shit," I breathed. It was almost midnight, and no one was around. I couldn't see anyone in the hall, and I knew I couldn't leave her like this.

The girl gasped and sat up. Her head lolled to one side and a trickle of saliva hit the carpet. "You," Her voice was raspy. "You. Listen."

I swallowed hard. This voice did not match her small frame. She was a china doll with the voice of a monster.

The girl coughed. "Listen. Something is happening. Nothing good will come of it." She reeled backwards. Her eyes were now wide and staring into nothingness. "Be warned, Bianca Hernandez. Those around you cannot be trusted. There are secrets. Secrets!" She convulsed and shuddered.

I looked around wildly and shouted, hoping someone, anyone, could hear me. "Help. Help we need a doctor!" I shrieked. "Help! Someone help!"

Just as my voice began to fail me, the lounge door was torn open. Ryland. I had never been so happy to see him before.

Ryland didn't say a word, watching the girl shuddering on the ground. "She's having a vision." He said. "Don't touch her."

"A vision?" I repeated.

"She's got Premonition," Ryland said as if that would mean anything to me. "She sees the future. It's a rare talent." He added.

I went cold. Was her prediction for me or was she just shouting nonsense? I edged away from her as the shaking turned violent again. "We need to call someone."

"She'll come out of it on her own."

"What? Dude, she's like fourteen. We can't just let this happen without reporting it!"

Ryland rolled his eyes. We hadn't spoken since our run-in at the gym and he had no reason to be kind to me. But this wasn't about me. It was for her. "Fine. Wait here, I'll use the emergency phone to call downstairs." He ran down the hall.

I waited, holding my breath.

Slowly, the girl's trembling stopped. She was panting and heaving. She began to cough and then vomited all over the floor.

I instinctively rolled her over onto her side, rubbing her back. "It's ok."

The girl screamed and pushed away from me, clawing at my skin. "Get away! Get away!" She stopped. With a sigh and a deep breath, her eyes refocused. She sat up and looked down at the vomit on her black dress. She spoke in a new voice, one that was soft and much more fitting. "Oh dear, I've made a mess, haven't I?"

The security guard came up a minute later with Ryland at his side. "What happened here?"

"A seizure," I said. I stood up so the guard could get down on her level and inspect the situation.

Ryland put a hand on my shoulder as we watched the security guard question her and take down some notes. "She'll be fine." His face was blank, as if he couldn't feel sympathy but he was trying to make me feel better anyways.

I glanced up at him. He was so hot and cold. I didn't know how to feel about him. Ryland was everything Luke wasn't; he was assertive while Luke compromised, determined when Luke was patient, aggressive where Luke was compassionate.

The security guard called housekeeping to get the mess cleaned up and helped the girl to her feet. "Hey," He barked at me. "Can you do me a favor and help her get washed and go to bed? I have all the details I need. She's alright."

I nodded and looked at the girl. Her black dress and long hair were covered in vomit. Her face was pale and sallow. Her eyes rimmed with dark circles. She looked, in a word, pathetic. My heart sank for her. "Of course," I said.

The guard took down Ryland's and my name and left.

"Do you need help?" Ryland asked.

I noticed he was in his gym clothes. He had probably been on the way down to the gym when he heard my calls. "No, I'm good. Just going to have some girl time," I joked. My laugh sounded forced. The girl didn't crack a smile.

Ryland shrugged. "Have it your way."

∞

"So, what's your name?" I asked the girl as she dried her hair.

"Katie White," She said in her soft angelic voice. She was wrapped in a fluffy white bathrobe and sitting in front of the mirror. Her pale skin and protruding cheekbones emphasized her dark eyes.

"Nice to meet you," I said. "I'm Bianca."

"Bianca," She said at the same time. "Yes, I know."

A chill ran down my spine. Did she know my name from the visions? No way. She heard me talking to the security guard. That was it.

"I've been having visions of you since you came on the first day. I saw you in the cafeteria." She said.

The chill turned into a full-on deep freeze. "What?" I breathed.

Katie shook her hair as she dried it. There were strands of gray running through it, despite her young age. "Do you remember what I said to you when I was in the vision? I have a hard time remembering details sometimes. Visions are like a dream; usually I can only grasp a few memories or feelings at a time."

"Uh," I said and clutched my knees so she wouldn't notice my hands shaking. "You said that there're secrets and no one I know should be trusted. You spoke my name. Told me to listen. Your voice didn't sound like you. It was deep and dark."

Katie set down her hairbrush. "Sounds about right." She stared at herself in the mirror. "I hope I didn't scare you too much."

"Honestly, you scared the shit out of me. But I'm glad I was there." I admitted.

Katie glanced down at my hands, noticing the scratches on them. "Word of advice for next time, don't touch someone while they're in a trance. We tend to come out of them terrified and violent. It's like waking up from a nightmare. People lash out." She reached out and touched the scratch; her hand was like ice.

I flinched.

"Sorry," Katie said and stuck her hands into the sleeves of the robe.

"It's ok," I said quickly. "Don't worry about it. I didn't know what to do. I thought you were having a seizure. There was no one around. It was scary. But I'm glad you're feeling better."

The corners of her lips turned up in a tiny smile. "Thanks for being there and calling security. Usually I'm alone when they happen. Could you walk me back to my room?"

"Of course," I said.

Katie piled her dirty clothes into a bag and pushed her feet into her fuzzy slippers. She also lived on the third floor, a few doors down the hall from me.

"Are you sure you're going to be alright?" I asked for the hundredth time that night.

Katie nodded. "Yeah. Just need to sleep." She paused, her key card inches from the door. "Bianca, about what I said while I was in the trance."

"Yes?"

Her voice was low and quiet, as if she was afraid even the walls could hear her. "Don't forget it. Something is happening. I don't know what. But whatever it is, it started with you."

CHAPTER SEVENTEEN

Good news broke on Monday afternoon — they found the student who had been teleporting with Ms. Blackwell. He had been located on the outskirts of the city by a highway patrol officer who got in touch with our agents. The entire school population breathed a sigh of relief as the news was shared over the speakers at lunch.

Questions filled the air: How did it happen? What went wrong? Was the teleportation ban going to be lifted? Was it safe to go out on field assignments?

Phylicia shook her head and let out a breath. "Thank goodness," She said.

I was equally as relieved. Since finding out about teleportation limbo, I decided there was nothing more terrifying than that. I saw

Katie across the room and gave her a little wave.

Phylicia watched us exchange smiles. "Who's that?"

"Katie," I said.

"Huh, look at you making new friends," Phylicia said. Her tone lowered. "Speaking of friends," She jerked her chin in the direction of the lunch buffet.

I turned around slightly to take a discrete peek. Ryland and Luke were there filling their plates. They looked as if they had just finished sparring; their hair was still wet from the shower.

"I don't know why the two of them are always together. They seem to hate each other," Phylicia whispered.

I shrugged. "Honestly, I don't know. They're both top of the class. No one can beat them. Doesn't the saying go: keep your friends close and your enemies closer?"

∞

"So, do you think you're ready for a field trip?" Professor Turner asked.

I let my hands fall to my sides. My fingers were tingling with pent up energy. I was moving objects with ease now and we had moved on to glass, which brought back scary memories. So far, I had cracked the glass, but the fear was holding me back.

"You mean *outside* of the academy?" I asked.

Turner scribbled some notes as he inspected the cracks in the glass. "Yes. With our missing student back safe and sound, I suspect the teleportation ban should be lifted shortly."

I rolled my shoulders and stretched. The buzzing hum of energy was rippling through my muscles, begging to be let loose again. "I suppose that wouldn't be so bad. When I'm ready." I added.

Professor Turner finished his notes. "You are an excellent student, Bianca," He said. "You've been working hard and overcome a lot of challenges during your short time at the Psychic Academy."

"Thank you, Professor Turner," I said as I adjusted my ponytail to avoid looking too awkward. He was standing so close to me. His cologne was the perfect blend of musk and spice.

"I told you, call me Jack." He said with a smile that oozed charm.

I let out an embarrassing giggle and then turned away and pretended to cough. I had never in my life felt comfortable enough to use a teacher's first name and I sure as hell would not start with *Professor Sexy*. "Sure," I said. "So, uh, where were we?"

"I was going to suggest that we let you train with the group." Turner said.

I swallowed hard. I hadn't sparred or trained with anyone before, unless I counted the incident at prom and I single-handedly ruined that.

"No need to be nervous," He added.

Wow, it was that obvious. I could never hide my emotions well. "Sure." I wiped my sweaty hands on my leggings. "Let's do it." My voice cracked with fake enthusiasm.

I followed Professor Turner through the narrow passages between the accordion walls into a larger room. There were half a dozen students training with various objects. Along the wall were more weights, rubber balls, and plastic orbs, among other standard exercise equipment.

"This group all have telekinetic powers. I was training them myself until the incident with Ms. Blackwell. Since then, they've been using this time to hone their skills until we find a replacement teacher."

"Replacement?"

"Only temporary. I assure you. Ms. Blackwell's recovery has been slow." His voice was void of sympathy.

I didn't reply, watching the six students working in pairs. They were tossing metal weights back and forth as if they were as light as air. They operated in perfect unison, their psychic bonds grabbing hold and letting go in some sort of game of catch. It was impressive, there was no doubt about it.

The students did not break concentration as we watched them and only stopped when Professor Turner snapped is fingers. "Alright class, I'd like to introduce you to our newest telekinetic talent." He put a hand on my shoulder. "Bianca Hernandez."

I recognized the faces from the cafeteria and the hall, but I didn't know any of them by name. There were two girls and four guys, all dressed in black training gear. The weights they had been using slowly sank to the floor as they looked me up and down.

"Hi," I said meekly. "Nice to meet you."

"Who would like to practice with our new recruit?" Turner asked.

No one stepped forward immediately, seeming very secure with their usual partners. Finally, a tanned boy with brown and blond spiked hair raised his hand. "I'll give it a go, sir."

"Qadir, thank you for volunteering." Turner said. "Be careful now, she is very talented." He beamed with pride and I prayed that I didn't totally screw up.

Qadir stopped at the middle of the mat and the other students backed away. "Ok, let's see what ya got, new girl." He smirked.

I already didn't like him. He was skinny and cocky and, if is ego was as big as his hair, totally not my kind of guy. I shook my hands out and stood in front of him. I did my best to ignore the other pairs of eyes that were watching us. I was determined not to make a fool of myself.

"Let's start with something simple." Turner picked up one of the plastic orbs and tossed it to Qadir, who didn't catch it with his hands, but with his mind.

If I wasn't so nervous, I would have been amazed. Qadir caught the orb mid flight, and it hovered above the ground, rotating slowly on its axis.

"Ready, new girl?" He smirked.

I bristled with anger. Wow, he was as annoying as I thought he'd be. "Ready." I said, but I felt nothing that could be remotely described as ready. I gasped as the orb flew towards me like a baseball. I flicked my wrist, and it flew off at a different angle.

"You're supposed to send it back to me. Not shoot it across the room." Qadir raised his hand, and the orb stopped. He flicked his fingers back towards me and the orb changed direction. It was moving at incredible speed. He was trying to get me to flinch.

I rooted myself in the ground and raised my hands. With my stance steady I was able to catch the orb this time. I extended my energy out and around the hard plastic. It hummed and vibrated but stayed still. I suppressed an excited shout and adjusted my power, so the orb came directly in front of me.

"Boring," My opponent drawled, and I felt a tug on my psychic connection. He was also connected to the orb, trying to pull it out of my invisible grasp.

I clenched my teeth and dug my heels into the mat. He was strong and my connection was slipping. I clenched my fists as if I could hang onto the orb with them. The plastic trembled and shook, flowing back and forth between us.

Qadir wasn't even straining. He slammed is foot down. The shock rang through my system and I lost control of the orb; it floated to him effortlessly. He caught it in his hand and shook his head.

"I thought you were powerful." He scoffed.

I bit back my response. I would not be embarrassed like that in front of my peers. Stretching my hand out, I regained my connection on the orb and tugged. I nearly pried it out of his hand.

Qadir laughed. "Nope, still not good enough." He wrenched it back from me.

"Screw off!" I shouted and a deep hum rolled through my body. The surrounding walls trembled.

I heard Professor Turner suck in a breath.

"You're not so great!" I summoned all my strength and pulled the orb away from him and sent it flying in the air.

Qadir's expression was priceless.

Suddenly, all the plastic orbs began to tremble on the floor. I was losing my cool and my connection was flickering. I felt a jolt of panic run through my body, but it was too late. There was a crackling sound and all the clear orbs shattered, sending pieces of plastic all over the room and raining down on us.

My heart sank before fear flooded my senses. I glanced at Turner, who looked as shocked as his six star students. The quiet settled around me. It was heavy and uncomfortable. They all looked at me as if I were a freak.

Holding back tears, I ran out of the training facility before anyone could stop me and didn't look back until I was in the garden. Alone at last.

I collapsed down on the bench, wiping hot messy tears from my face. My chest heaved, and every breath came out as a shudder. This was my "ugly crying" that only Daniel and Jessica knew how to deal with. In that moment my heart ached for them. I missed my friends so much it was unbearable. Being alone like this sucked.

My Disney-princess-style pity party was cut short by the sound of footsteps on the garden path.

I bolted up, wiping the tears from my face with my sleeve. Thank goodness I didn't wear makeup tonight or else I would have looked like a half-melted panda.

"Bianca." It was Professor Turner. He looked softer, almost boyish with his hands in his pockets, leaning on one hip. "I'm sorry, that shouldn't have happened." In all the excitement, his usual slicked back hair had come loose. Strands fell into his eyes and he flicked them back.

I shrugged. "Whatever."

"It's not whatever." He gestured to the bench. "May I?"

I edged over to the other side to make room for him but said nothing.

"I didn't mean for that to happen." Turner continued. "I thought you were ready to train with others."

"Guess not," I muttered.

"No, you are," He insisted. "But the choice of partner was my mistake. I underestimated Qadir's obsession with proving himself. I shouldn't have let you work with him." He paused. "I hope this didn't dampen your spirits too much."

I let out a harsh chuckle as I wiped more tears from my eyes. "I don't think anything could make me feel more self conscious than everything that's happened to me over the last few weeks. I'm trying. I really am."

"I know that." Turner put a hand on my shoulder. His grip was tight but comforting. "Trust me, Bianca, you're going to be great. Just keep at it. You need to believe in yourself."

A warmth blossomed in my chest. "Do you really think so?"

Professor Turner touched my cheek and turned me to face him. "I know so."

My heart skipped a beat, sending me into dangerous territory. He was nearly twice my age. He was my professor. He was so off limits. Why did I want to fall into his arms? I had never ever had a thing for older guys, but he was different somehow. I lowered my lashes and looked away.

"Bianca," Turner said. "I know that we have a professional relationship, but I need to tell you something."

I held my breath, unable to look him in the eye.

"You will be amazing. Trust me. I know that you've had a rough time with this but believe me when I say that you are exceptional." He wrapped his arm around me and held me close.

I didn't budge. I wanted to feel his strength. I wanted to surrender to him and just feel safe for a moment longer.

My bliss was cut off by the sound of the dinner bell. My heart pained as he let me go. "Thanks," I said without being sure what exactly I was thanking him for.

"Don't mention it. We'll try again tomorrow," Turner said. "And as soon as the Major lifts the teleportation ban, we're going to see what you can really do, Bianca."

CHAPTER EIGHTEEN

Thanks to the quasi-abandoned expanse of old warehouses that littered the edge of the Detroit River, we didn't need to go far from the academy to get some field work in. In fact, much to my relief, we didn't even teleport.

We, Professor Turner, myself, and Ryland, arrived at an old shipping yard. The warehouse looked like it hadn't been used in years. The enormous shipping containers sat stacked in neat piles, as if waiting for a ship that never arrived. The bright security lighting gave it an eerie feel.

"What if someone sees us?" I wondered out loud.

"Don't worry about that, these cameras have been dysfunctional for months." Ryland said.

I whipped my head around to look at him. "No offense, but why are you here?"

Ryland scoffed and crossed his arms. His twin daggers dangled at his sides. "Security, obviously. Teacher-student pairs need a third wheel until the Major loosens his ban on traveling outside the academy."

And of course, he had to be partnered with me. I was itching to repair what had gone wrong that night in the gym, even though I was more focused on building a relationship with Luke. That was easier said than done with his intense schedule. With Ms. Blackwell out, that left only one qualified teleportation professor, and Luke had been called in to pick up the slack until they could find a replacement. I hoped they were paying him at least.

"Alright, why don't we get started?" Professor Turner said. He waved Ryland back. Turner did not seem happy to have a third wheel either. He looked at Ryland with contempt. "Young man, just try to stay out of the way."

Ryland gritted his teeth and his jaw flexed angrily. "Fine." He spat.

Turner motioned for me to stand in front of him. We were enclosed in a clearing between the shipping containers stacked three high, shielded from any curious onlookers who were very unlikely to be around in the first place.

The moon shone bright and full above us. I wished we didn't have to go train at night. I shook my hands and let the tension unwind from my shoulders and back. This was no time to be worried about being caught. I was with one of the academy's best teachers and one of the best students. I was in very capable hands.

Turner looked handsome in the glowing moonlight. I forced those thoughts away; he was my teacher. He was only my teacher. I couldn't harbor these childlike fantasies if I was going to get control of my powers. I couldn't be distracted by anything.

"Tonight, we're going to release the power you've been holding back." Professor Turner said. "Let go of your fear and use the powers the flow within you."

I heard Ryland suck in a breath, but I ignored him. He too, had told me how powerful I was, despite being barely able to move a ball until recently. I didn't believe him then, but lately I was realizing that maybe my skills far surpassed my low expectations. I had never really been good at anything before; this new realization gave me hope that just maybe I would be someone who was better than average at something — anything.

"Bianca, can you tell me about the first few times your powers revealed themselves?"

I hesitated, gathered my thoughts, and nodded. "I was in dangerous situations or feeling anxious. Anger and fear seemed to be my triggers. Now I'm much more in control."

"I want you to let go of that control. No one can get hurt here. No one can see us. I need you to let go and feel your power. It's in there, hiding and suppressed. You'll do no one any favors by ignoring your potential." Turner raised his hand and a large piece of twisted metal skidded between us. "Glass was too easy. Let's try something a bit more challenging."

I looked down at the metal sheet. It was warped as if it had been held in the fist of a giant. The sound it made when it dragged along the asphalt emphasized how dense and heavy the materials were.

I held out my hands with my palms facing the metal. I twisted my heels into the ground and breathed deeply. I could summon the feeling with ease now; I let the powers trickled from my head, down my spine, through my arms and to my fingertips. My hands twitched with energy. My powers were an extension of myself. All I had to do was focus on what I wanted to do, and my psychic energy would obey. The familiar tingle at the base of my head returned.

I sucked in a breath, braced my body and flung my energy at the metal. The sheet rose into the air and groaned under its own weight. I strained, psychically feeling the heaviness in my mind. My hands trembled.

"I want you to twist it," Turner said.

I clenched my fists as if I were wringing out a towel. With a creak, the metal bowed to my command and twisted as easily as tinfoil. I gasped, and the metal fell to the ground with a bang. I slumped down to the ground, my vision blurred, and my stomach knotted.

When I recovered from the wave of exhaustion, I looked up to see Professor Turner smiling at me. "Excellent work. Next time try not to drop it so suddenly. You need to control when you get tired; don't panic. Your body can endure more than you think."

I smiled back and fell backwards onto my butt. I stretched out my legs and wiped the sweat from my forehead. "I can't believe I did that."

"Catch your breath, and you'll do it again," Turner said. He walked over to the metal plate to take notes.

Ryland sat down beside me. "That was cool," He said. "I'm actually impressed."

I guess that was his way of complimenting me. "Thanks," I said with a shrug. My body was drained from the effort it took to twist hundreds of pounds of metal.

"Bianca, I," Ryland started. "I wanted to apologize to how I've been towards you. I really like you. You're amazing and I want you to know that I never—" He was cut off by the sound of cackling.

The voice was all too familiar to me. It was that greasy Rogue that just couldn't seem to stay away from me. I bit down on my cheek and looked up. He was standing on the double-stacked shipping containers, dressed in a tattered trench coat. Seriously, was he trying to look like a one-bit DC villain? (Daniel would have been proud of that comparison.)

"Hello, little girl. We meet again."

Yep. This guy definitely read too many comics.

"Leave me alone!" My voice surprised me. I wasn't scared anymore, not with my increased skill and with Ryland by my side. I jumped to my feet; I forgot my exhaustion after the rush of adrenaline.

Ryland was at the ready, both daggers in hand. "I'm not letting him escape a third time," He said through gritted teeth.

"Who are you?" Professor Turner shouted.

"Don't worry about me, Professor," The Rogue psychic laughed. The ground rumbled beneath our feet and the shipping containers vibrated against the asphalt.

For a greasy loser, he sure was powerful. But it was three against one.

"Bianca, we need to tire him out so he can't teleport away. That's the only way we're going to stop him." Ryland whispered.

I nodded. "Ok, let's do it."

"My head is telling me you should sit this one out, but we don't have an option. We need all the power we can get. So, just, don't get hurt, alright?"

Ryland needed to work on showing how he cared. I knew what he was getting at, but why did everything need to sound so back handed? "Don't worry about me," I insisted. "This guy has bothered me for the last time." I clenched my fists and let my energy surge forward.

The man threw his hands forward, and the ground trembled beneath us with enough force to leave cracks running through the asphalt like a dark spiderweb. "Come on, kids, let's have some fun."

"Bianca! Ryland!" The professor shouted over the sounds of the ground cracking beneath us. "Be careful, he's not going to go down easy."

"No kidding," Ryland said under his breath. He narrowed his eyes. "There's something blocking my ability to read his mind," He said, visibly frustrated. "You and Turner are going to have to trap him."

I threw up my arms and sent the twisted metal sheet flying towards the man. He disappeared and reappeared to dodge it. I grunted, lassoing my powers on the metal mid-flight and sending it back towards him. He barely dodged that one. I held onto the metal like some sort of psychic ball and chain. Sweat ran into my eyes as I forced the sheet towards him one more time before losing my connection. It crashed to the ground.

"Excellent work, Bianca," Turner said. He flicked his wrists and used his powers to grab the metal where it fell. With one smooth motion, he knocked the man off the shipping containers.

There was a crunch when he landed, but he seemed unfazed. The man scoffed. "So annoying," He groaned and turned his attention on the Professor. "Stay out of this!" He raised his hand.

Professor Turner rose into the air, as if he were being held by an invisible hand. He strained and struggled to breathe.

"Professor Turner!" I shouted. "Let him go!"

The greasy guy clenched his fist tighter and Turner let out an agonized groan. He gasped for air as his rips popped under the pressure. With a flick of his wrist, the man sent Turner flying backwards.

Turner rolled to a stop and didn't move. His handsome face was bleeding.

I only had a moment before my fear turned to seething anger. "That's it." I growled low in my throat.

"Bianca, be careful, think before you act!" Ryland shouted.

I didn't need to think anymore. I needed to feel. I needed to do the opposite of Ms. Blackwell had taught what me. Being calm and in control wouldn't help me against this enemy. He had hurt enough people. He was ruthless; I would be, too.

I clenched my fists and connected myself to as many scrap pieces of metal that I could. My voice ripped out of me as I pushed with all my might and flung them at him. The shards of metal circled around him, trapping my enemy in a vortex of scraps of aluminum, iron, and tin.

"Holy shit," Ryland breathed.

The greasy man shouted. Nothing came out of his mouth but a waterfall of profanities. He was trapped, and he knew it. He held up his arms to shield his face. "You little bitch!"

I had to stop him before he teleported himself out. With a flick of my fingers I sent the smaller shards towards him, cutting and biting at his skin.

The man was having trouble keeping his levitation steady. I could sense the energy fading from him.

"Now, while he's weak!" Ryland shouted. He was at my side and holding my shoulders steady.

I blinked sweat away from my eyes and clenched my fists. The metal groaned and creaked, forming a solid cage around him. I brought the cage down to the ground with a clatter. Inside, the man was unconscious.

I let out a shaking breath and collapsed against Ryland. My knees were shaking, and my stomach was turning with nausea.

Ryland slowly laid me down on the ground. "You were amazing," He said, brushing my hair away from my face. "I've never seen anything like that before. I knew you were powerful but, wow, that was something else. You are something special, Bianca."

Maybe it was just my exhaustion, but there was something different about him. His eyes glowed with an emotion I had never seen in him before: Pride? Adoration? I wasn't sure how to label it. I struggled to sit up.

"No, no," Ryland said gently. "Save your strength." He nestled me in his arms and stared into my eyes. He leaned in a kissed me tenderly.

I didn't resist. My hand shook as it held onto his; being in his arms felt so right.

There was a groan.

We both bolted up, our adrenaline surging, but the man was still knocked out.

The groan was from Professor Turner. He struggled to his feet and looked around in disbelief. "Did you? How?" He shook his head, eyes wide at the surrounding scene.

"We got him," I said.

"Well, she got him, more like," Ryland said and winked at me.

I shrugged it off. My mother had raised me to be modest, and it didn't seem right to take all the credit. "Either way, we're safe now."

Turner's eyes were dark. He frowned as he inspected the man and his metal enclosure. "How did you do this?" He ran his finger along the cage. The different metals twisted together smoothly; it looked unnaturally beautiful.

"I don't know," I said. Ryland helped me regain my balance when my wobbling legs threatened to give out. "I just felt angry, and I did it."

Turner smirked and nodded as he appraised my handiwork. "Well, this was unexpected," He muttered under his breath.

I wasn't sure what he meant by that, but I was too tired to care.

Ryland pulled a walkie-talkie out of his pocket. "I will call to get us teleported out of here." His voice sounded far away.

I blinked, and the scene faded to darkness as I finally gave into exhaustion.

CHAPTER NINETEEN

When I woke up, I was in the nurse's office. The walls were white; the lights were bright, and everything smelled like bleach. I gasped. "What happened?"

"Don't worry, I got you." Ryland was sitting beside my bed.

I eased back into the not-so-comfortable bed. The room was small, and we were alone.

"You passed out back there. I called for back up and we were teleported back safely." Ryland sat back in his chair and shook my head. "You gave us all a scare."

"Why?"

"You've been asleep for over a day."

My jaw dropped. "What?"

"Over twenty nine hours to be exact." A woman walked in. I could safely assume she was the academy nurse based on her scrubs and clipboard. "Let's check your vitals and get some food in you."

Before I could object, she was already checking my pulse. I didn't have the energy to refuse anyway. I let her do her "nurse stuff" and was rewarded with a big bowl of soup.

The room lit up as the rising sun's rays streamed through the window. I had missed an entire day to sleep. It felt so wrong. And what was worse, I felt the opposite of well-rested. My head ached and my stomach was queasy.

Ryland watched me eat and told me what I had missed in the past day. "We caught the guy, thanks to you. He was still unconscious when the authorities arrived. I'm sure you can imagine how hard it is to apprehend someone with teleportation powers, they were amazed." He brushed my hand lightly. "You're really something, Bianca."

I blushed. I had always been terrible at taking compliments. As much as it was against my nature, I really had to agree with him on this one. I kicked ass that night; I even surprised myself. "What did they do?"

"He's been arrested by the special FBI division. He won't be bothering us again." Ryland said. His expression was hard.

Relief flooded me. I took another sip of hot soup before asking my next question. "Is Professor Turner alright?"

"Yeah, he's fine aside from a few bruises and a fractured rib," Ryland said with a shrug.

I didn't miss the change in his tone. "What's wrong?"

Ryland frowned; his eyes focused somewhere in the distance. "I just don't trust him."

"Trust him? Why wouldn't you?"

"I can't say for sure."

"Have you tried getting into his head?"

Ryland glanced behind him to make sure the nurse was gone. "Yeah, but we're strictly forbidden to use our powers against teachers. I haven't been able to get a good latch on him and I know he'll sense it if I do." He shook his head. "Whatever. It's probably nothing. Just be careful around him, alright?"

I nodded and quietly finished my soup.

Ryland sat with me, seemingly unbothered by the silence.

We both spoke at the same time.

"Ryland, about the kiss last night."

"Bianca, about the kiss last night."

We both stop and chuckled. I looked away and shook my head.

Ryland spoke first. "I wanted to say that I really liked kissing you. But I'm sorry if you didn't want it. You weren't in the right mind."

Wait. Was he — Ryland - effing - Willams — actually fumbling over his words? Was he apologizing to me? No way. I must have woken up in some alternate universe.

I raised a finger and pressed it to his lips to silence him. "It's ok. I liked it," I said with a smile. "It was really good. Confusing. But good."

"Confusing?" Ryland repeated. He lifted his hand up to entangle our fingers together. It felt good. It felt right.

I chuckled softly. "I mean, I still don't know how I feel about you, Ryland. It might have just been the moment, but I really liked you kissing me. And, honestly, I really liked you kissing me in the gym too. But," I trailed off.

"You thought I was in your head, didn't you?"

I nodded.

Ryland sighed and rolled his shoulders. "Bianca, I swear to you. I would never use my powers against you like that," He said. "Besides. I can't read your mind. It's as if something is blocking it."

"How can I block it? I don't know anything like that."

Ryland shook his head. "I don't know. But what I do know is that I was right about sensing great power in you. Your psychic energy must block me somehow." He paused. "Remember that night in the park when Luke and I saved you and your little friend?"

"Daniel," I corrected. "Yeah. Why?"

"Remember when I transmitted a message into your head?"

I paused to think. *Tell no one what you saw.* So, it had been him. "Yes! I remember!"

Ryland nodded and held my hand a little tighter. "That was the hardest thing I had to do in a long time. It was like swimming in oil." He blinked, wondering if I got the analogy, and continued when I nodded. "Slipping into minds is effortless for me. But not when it comes to you." He gestured around the room. "I can get into anyone's head in this academy. You're the only one who's a mystery to me, Bianca. I want to get to know you better. I know I was a jerk to you before, but please give me another chance."

I took a moment to consider his words. Despite feeling welcomed in the Psychic Academy, there was an unbearable loneliness that I couldn't shake. Would it be so bad to give Ryland a second chance?

I didn't answer him with words. I leaned in and kissed him. He tensed in response and then melted against me, cupping my cheek with his hand and running his thumb against my jaw. The kiss turned hot and needy.

I edged over on the bed and he took me in his arms. I straddled either side of the chair, holding onto his shoulders as he kissed my jawline and neck.

I was naked under the hospital gown, not even wearing panties. His hands roamed down my waist, over my thighs and up the hem of the pastel green fabric. My body ached with need. I wanted his touch. I wanted his kisses all over my body. Right here. Right now.

The sound of the door opening jerked us back into reality. I sprang backwards on the bed with more energy than I should have had. Ryland stood up and straightened his shirt. We were both panting when the nurse came in.

"Bianca, I've finished your paperwork, you can return to the dormitories and resume class tomorrow." The nurse said in her brisk and business-like tone. If she had any idea of what she interrupted, it didn't show.

I nodded. "Great." Maybe I could get back to the dorms with Ryland and finish what we started.

"And speaking of classes," The nurse added. "The Major called me. He told me to remind you that waiting at her bedside was honorable, but you have a midterm next week and better get to class, Mr. Williams."

Ryland shrugged. "Alright, I'm going." He looked over his shoulder and winked at me. "See you later, Bianca." He said and shut the door behind him.

∞

The dormitory was quiet during class hours. I showered and bummed around in my room for a little while before going out to the lounge to see if there was another soul to make the time pass quicker.

Finding the lounge empty, I picked a DVD at random, turned on the television and flopped down on the couch. Titanic would kill three hours and then it would be time for dinner.

About halfway through the movie, Katie White came in. She made a surprised peep that reminded me of a kitten.

I tried not to look overly enthusiastic about having company. The loneliness and quiet had been eating away at me since leaving the nurse's office. "Hi, Katie."

She looked at me shyly. "Hi. Do you mind if I sit with you?"

"Sure." I curled up my legs so there was room for her.

"I heard about what happened. I'm glad you're ok," Katie said.

It didn't surprise me in the least. I was positive everyone at the academy knew about the incident. It was embarrassing. "Oh?" I feigned surprise. "What did they say?"

"That you got attacked by some Rogue Psychic," She said.

"It wasn't so bad." I shrugged it off and tried to change the subject, but she kept talking.

"That won't be the last time."

A shiver ran through my body. "What?"

"I told you. You're powerful. Something is going on. Someone wants you." Katie said.

I hugged my knees to my chest, only then noticing that my socks didn't match. Maybe I wasn't as well rested as I thought. "Yeah, you said that," I mumbled.

Katie forced a smile in my direction. I could tell that it was an expression she rarely made. "Listen, I'll do my best to tell you if I sense any danger if you promise to do your best not to get hurt. Or worse."

"Noted." I swallowed hard. "Why are you looking out for me, anyway?"

"Because you stayed with me while I was having an episode," Katie said. "You know how often I wake up scared and alone in my own puke? It's a nightmare. Everyone who's been here for a while doesn't even care anymore."

I remembered Ryland's cold, indifferent reaction. I shook my head. "I could never leave someone like that."

"You're a good person," Katie whispered as she picked at the hem of her t-shirt. "That's why I want to help you."

"I appreciate that," I said with a sigh. "I just hope it's no more trouble than it's worth." If that Rogue was only the beginning, what else was coming my way?

"It's about time I use my powers for something," Katie said with a cynical chuckle.

"What do you mean?" I sat up straight so I could face her properly. There was a glimmer of sadness in her eyes.

Katie shrugged. "I have what they call a 'passive talent'. Which means I'm not much good at fighting or anything like that. Kids with active talents, like you, get way more attention. If the passive kids can't prove themselves in physical training, we're just seen as a waste of time."

That must have been why she finished class before dinner and why I had never seen her in any of the training labs. "Hey, your talent is far from useless! "

She shrugged again. "I can see the future but only at the whims of my talent. I can't control it yet."

"You're still young, give it time," I said as if I had some sort of clue. I was new to this too. "I'm sure the psychic world needs people like you."

"Well, my other talent is finding lost stuff. Clairvoyance. So, I always figured I'd work for the police or something in the future. Not that they'd want a weakling like me." She lifted her pale hands and twisted her bony wrists to emphasize the fact.

"I know a clairvoyant who works for the FBI," I said. "I'm sure they'd be thrilled to have someone with your set of skills."

That seemed to perk her up a little. She curled her legs underneath her and pulled her hands into her over-sized sweater. "That's good news." Katie leaned her head against the arm of the sofa. "I never really liked having powers." She whispered so faintly I wasn't sure if she was speaking to me or not.

"I'm sure it's stressful," I said. I couldn't quite imagine what it must be like at such a young age to be away from her parents haunted by premonitions. It explained her introverted behavior. "But if you ever need me, I'll be here."

"I hope so." Katie's simple words shattered my confidence once again.

CHAPTER TWENTY

Sadly, Ryland never showed up that evening to finish what we started in the nurse's room. It was probably for the best; I told myself. I knew better than to get caught up between Ryland and Luke. I still couldn't decide who was best for me. Luke was so nice and caring and understanding, Ryland was just so... exciting. I always had a soft spot for bad boys.

There was still an hour before curfew, so I went to the training facility to burn off some steam. I threw on black leggings and a tank top, grabbed a bottle of water, and tied my shoelaces tight.

The lounges were filled with students and even the grounds had a few groups soaking up the rays of the setting sun. I didn't run into anyone I knew on my way to the training facility, though I got a few curious glances. I had no doubt that the entire academy knew what had happened, as Katie had alluded to.

When I arrived at the training facility all the accordion walls had been retracted, leaving the enormous room open and flooded with white fluorescent light. Only two people were there, positioned at the very center of the room. Ryland and Luke. I couldn't believe my luck.

Before I could back out and slip away, they both noticed me and looked in my direction. Their tense poses eased a fraction.

"Bianca?" Luke raised his eyebrows. "Shouldn't you be resting?"

"I've done enough resting," I forced out, trying to be heard across the distance. The facility's acoustics were terrible.

Luke flickered out of sight and reappeared at my side. "There, now you don't have to yell."

I gasped and took a step back. "Please warn me before you do that!"

"That's not the point of being able to teleport." He laughed and shook his head.

Luke's warm smile always put butterflies in my stomach, the same way that Ryland's smoldering scowl made my chest tight.

"You should rest," Ryland said. He jogged over. His twin daggers clattered against his belt. "The nurse didn't clear you until tomorrow."

"Yeah, yeah," I waved away his concern even though it flattered me. "I can't sleep. I needed to do something." I pulled the elastic off my wrist and gathered my long hair into a ponytail. "So, who's first?"

Luke gulped and Ryland's face went red.

I coughed to hide my embarrassed squeak. "I meant for sparring." I amended my vaguely inviting statement. "Geez, guys, get you heads out of the gutter. I just woke up from a not-so-literal coma."

"Which is exactly why you shouldn't be sparring!" Ryland argued. He was adorable when he showed that he cared.

"Fine." I planted my hands on my hips. "So, can I watch you guys?"

Luke and Ryland exchanged glances as if they were thinking the same thing. For guys who openly disliked each other, they sure were amazing partners in battle. Maybe I wasn't the only one who couldn't make up their mind in this crazy place.

"Well, we were just about to pack up," Luke said, tipping his head.

"Ah, come on. Let's give the lady a show." Ryland was always eager to fight and show off his skills. He glanced at the clock. "We still have forty-five minutes left, may as well make the most of it."

"You mean forty-five minutes for me to kick your ass again," Luke bit back, bracing his body.

I didn't miss the hard muscle flexing beneath his training clothes. I suddenly felt hot, even with the air conditioning in full blast. These two boys would be the death of me if I didn't pick one of them soon.

With a shout, Ryland drew his blades and ran at Luke. Luke disappeared with a pop and reappeared over his opponent. Ryland was quick; he dodged the kick and rolled out from underneath him. They continued in a what looked to be a well-choreographed dance. They knew each other's weak spots and advantage points. They worked together like a machine.

Luke dodged and was hit by Ryland. "Ah, shit!" He stumbled back.

"Gotta keep your guard up," Ryland taunted and twirled his blades. They were dull daggers meant for training, not like the ones he brought to a real fight; I had no doubt they could still do serious damage.

"Get the hell out of my head." Luke pinched his nose and spat blood onto the mat.

"You never were good at blocking your thoughts. All this time and I can still read you like a book." Ryland laughed.

"And yet I still beat you every time."

Ryland's grin faded into a frown. "Enough talk. Come at me."

I watched them surge forward and clash again. They fought so fast that their arms and legs were like blurs. I didn't know anything about martial arts, but I'd bet these two could give any black belt a run for their money.

The fight ended with Ryland on his back. He groaned and tapped out.

Luke smirked and offered a hand to help him up.

Ryland refused. He glanced at me, but instead of his usual dashing grin or seductive smirk, his expression was like that of a wounded dog.

"Ryland, are you ok?" I ran to his side.

Ryland shrugged me off and brushed back his blond hair. "Never better. See you later." He didn't look back as he left the training room, his daggers hanging loose from his hands.

"He'll be fine," Luke said, wiping the sweat from his face. "Ryland's always been a sore loser. Especially when he loses in front of a pretty girl."

The compliment didn't register until a moment later. "Pretty girl?"

"Yeah, you." Luke said. He paused to take a sip of water. "I know how you look at him. He's way much charming than me. I wouldn't blame you if you chose me over him."

I held in a gasp. "What? Who said anything about—"

Luke shook his head to silence me. "Don't spare my feelings, Bianca," He said. "I may have only known Ryland for a few months, but I know that most girls would pick him over me. Good guys finish last." He chuckled dryly and sighed.

"That's not true." I protested and touched his shoulder.

"So, you're saying I still have a chance?" He raised his eyebrows.

When he said it like that it sounded so bad. I didn't want to compete for feelings. I wasn't special enough that two guys should care about me like they both did. My entire life I had never been anyone's romantic conquest aside from a few crushes and guys with a "Asian fetish" (barf, I didn't even want to think about that).

"What I'm saying is," I started, choosing my words carefully. "I don't want to have to make a choice right now. Right now, I just want to know who's after me. Why did that Rogue attack me? Is Ms. Blackwell doing ok?"

Luke nodded, silent in thought. "Well, I can't solve all your problems. But I can help with one."

"What's that?" I perked up.

"I can take you to see Ms. Blackwell."

"What? How?"

Luke lowered his voice and glanced around. "Just meet me at the teleportation area tomorrow after class."

∞

I was crazy for going through with this. Teleportation had only been approved if students were traveling with a professor for educational purposes only. We had neither of those requirements met.

Luke was already waiting there when I arrived. He was dressed in casual jeans and a t-shirt. I had dressed similarly. We needed to look as inconspicuous as possible.

The gates were locked, and the lights were off. A quick glance around confirmed that no one was around, and I hadn't been followed.

"So, how are we going to do this?" I whispered.

"The academy has certain technological protections against teleportation," Luke explained. "This is the only point in which people can teleport in and out. It's normally tightly monitored, but it has been seriously lacking lately."

"Why?" I asked.

Luke shrugged. "I suspect it has something to do with Ms. Blackwell being off duty and teleportation being banned without a teacher."

"So how are we going to get away with this?"

Luke pulled a tiny pin off the waistband of his jeans. "When we travel, students are marked with one of these. Those with teleportation talents are monitored 24-7."

I cringed. "That sucks."

Luke shrugged again and tossed the pin across the yard. "We'll only be gone for an hour. No one will suspect a thing." He offered his hand to me. "Ready?"

"Ready." I held my breath and touched his hand.

There was an immense pressure and a pop sound. It felt as if I was enduring the worst turbulence of my life. As quickly as it started, it ended. I shook myself and closed my eyes to wait out the dizziness. "I thought I'd be used to this by now."

"It takes a while." Luke said apologetically. "You're doing well. I give you bonus points for not puking. I think this is the furthest you've gone."

I opened my eyes and looked around. We were in a hospital; I could tell by the bland paint and weird smell. I hated how hospitals smelled. Luke had teleported us in an empty waiting room. I made a mental note to ask him how the hell he did this stuff without getting caught once we were safely back; I didn't want to jinx him.

"Come on, she's in room 715." Luke said.

The halls were generally quiet for a weekday afternoon. Nurses and doctors gave us brief smiles as we passed, and no one stopped to ask us why we were here. Many of the rooms were empty.

As if sensing the dozens of questions running through my head, Luke answered me. "We're in a special ward for psychic injuries. These nurses and doctors are specialized. It's top secret."

I guess that explained why he was so comfortable teleporting in here. I shook my head and added this to my ever-growing list of things I didn't quite understand. It amazed me that so many things were hidden right under the noses of ordinary citizens; at least I wasn't alone in my complicated lies.

I followed him to room 715. It was dark inside and silent, except for the beeping of a heart monitor.

Luke didn't knock, instead walking straight in and gently pulling aside the curtains to reveal the bed where Ms. Blackwell lay.

My heart panged when I saw her.

Ms. Blackwell was lying in a hospital gown and layers of blankets were piled to her chest. She had a breathing tube and several other wires connected all over. The machines monitored her breathing, her heartbeat, and her brain waves. She looked old and frail somehow; she was a pale shadow of the woman that I both feared and admired.

"Oh." A soft sound escaped my lips. I held my hands to my chest, unable to ignore the pain that was spreading from my heart.

Luke nodded solemnly. "I saw her as soon as the ban was eased, with the Major's permission, of course." He shook his head. "She's been in a coma since that night. No one has any idea what happened to her or if someone else is at fault. The student who was found doesn't remember a thing."

I clenched my fists. It didn't sound like an accident. I'd bet that someone had attacked them just like they had attacked me. I forced myself to look away from her. "Will she come out soon?"

Luke shrugged. "Your guess is as good as mine."

I shook my head. "I don't want to be here anymore."

I walked back out into the blinding light of the hallway, blinking away tears. What emotion was this? It wasn't quite sadness; it was mixed with frustration and helplessness. Somehow, I felt like the blame was on me. Had the same Rogue had attacked her? I slammed my fist against the wall and the picture frames began to tremble because of my surging energy.

"Hey, don't lose your cool." Luke was at my side immediately.

I hadn't noticed that the chairs were floating around me. I sighed, and they fell back to the floor with a control that I hadn't expected with my mind in this state. I took half a second to be proud of myself before sinking to the ground and hugging my knees.

"I'm sorry you had to see that," Luke said and sat down beside me.

The tiled floor was cold. "No, I'm glad you did. I just didn't expect it to hurt so much."

"People create bonds in the academy. Some unlike any other bond I've ever experienced in my life. Ms. Blackwell is more than a teacher to me. She's a mentor and a friend. I hope one day to be as half as powerful as she is. I know you've only seen her kinetic skills, but her teleportation and apportation skills are even more impressive."

I didn't doubt that. I watched a nurse pass by before speaking. "I would have never guessed that discovering these powers would cause so much pain." I choked back a sob.

Luke waved his hand and a tissue box disappeared from a nearby cart and reappeared in his hand. He offered me a tissue, which I gladly accepted.

"I know what you mean. I used to wish every day that I never developed the powers I had. It took me a long time to adjust, even with a psychic parent. But truth is, I always had powers, they didn't just appear one day. So did you. Maybe they manifested themselves in little ways and other times they were silent, but they were always a part of you."

I blew my nose and considered his words. "Now that you mention it, I always had a weird knack at guessing who was calling. Even before caller ID was mainstream." I added with a laugh.

"Maybe there's a hint of clairvoyance in you too." Luke mused.

"Maybe," I said with a shrug. "If I did, I'd use it to help find out what happened to Ms. Blackwell."

"Don't lose hope." Luke forced a smile that echoed my own worries. "Come on, let's get back before someone notices we're gone."

We teleported out of the hospital and back to the academy without incident. The sky was getting dark when we popped back into the designated area.

My vision blurred, but the dizziness was bearable.

Luke went off to look for his pin he threw away earlier. "Probably wasn't the best idea." He mumbled to himself.

I helped him comb through the grass near the fence. A minute later, I found the small metal pin and held it up victoriously. I inspected it carefully. "Luke, did you say all students who leave the campus for training have to wear these?"

Luke nodded as he took it from me. "Yep. And those who have the ability to teleport have to wear it all the time. A bit extreme if you ask me." He secured it on his waistband.

"Hm." I looked at my hands as I thought. I didn't remember wearing one when Professor Turner had taken me out to practice. He hadn't mentioned tracking at all; neither had Ryland.

"What's up?" Luke asked, noticing my furrowed brow.

"I didn't wear one when I went out and got attacked. Professor Turner didn't even mention it."

Luke's eyes widened. "That's not allowed. He would have got in major trouble. Are you sure?"

I nodded. "I'd never seen one until today."

Luke's expression darkened. "Who did you say was with you that night?"

"Ryland and the professor."

"Something's not right. You go out without trackers and conveniently get attacked?" Luke paced back and forth as he spoke.

"Do you think it was intentional?" I asked.

"All I know right now is that I don't know who to trust in this school." Luke put a hand on my shoulder. "Be careful, Bianca. And don't go anywhere with Turner or Ryland."

I gasped at his accusation. "You think Ryland could be behind this?"

Luke chose his words carefully as he spoke. "I wouldn't put it past him. Did he ever tell you why he got transferred from the west coast? He has a history."

"No way. He wouldn't try to hurt me." I tried my hardest to believe my words, but how could I be sure? I didn't really know him better that anyone else in this school. I had no reason to believe that he wouldn't be out to get me, aside from the times he had saved me.

"He's your partner," I added. "Surely you know him better than me. You know that he wouldn't hurt me. How many times have you guys saved my ass?"

"Doesn't matter. Somehow that Rogue knew exactly where you would be. Again." Luke stressed the last word with a pointed glance. He looked out in the distance. "It's important for you to know that there are forces at work behind the scenes that most students don't even think about. It wouldn't surprise me that someone within our walls was collaborating with the Rogues."

A chill ran down my spine. "Well, it that's the case, we just need to find out who did it before anyone else gets hurt."

"You make it sound so easy," Luke said with a dry chuckle.

"I don't want anyone else to get hurt. Please, tell me if you find any clues."

Luke considered my words. The silence stretched between us. "Fine. I promise I'll tell you if I hear anything but promise me, you'll stay out of trouble."

I nodded. "Promise."

Luke grabbed my hands and held them to his chest. "I know that we have more important things to worry about, but I just want to be with you." He sighed. "Do you think once this is all over and we get proper teleportation rights back, we could get that pizza in Chicago?"

I smiled and the warmth from his hands spread to my heart. "Luke, I would like that very much." I kissed his cheek.

Once this was over, I swore to myself that I would figure out what was going on in my heart. Until then, I just had to wait it out and see.

CHAPTER TWENTY ONE

There was no way I would believe that Ryland was behind any of the strange events that were happening. Sure, he was far from perfect; he was quite honestly a bit of a jerk most of the time. But I somehow knew deep in my heart that there was no way he would be involved with something as evil as attacking the academy students and professors.

Instead of moping in my room all night to think about it, I decided to go right to the source. I threw on some shorts and a tank top, tied my hair and went down to the gym to blow off some steam. I figured that Ryland would show up down there eventually, and then I would get him to talk.

When I arrived, there were two guys using the rowing machines and a girl stretching on a yoga mat. I ignored them and headed over to the treadmill. Over the past few weeks I had been able to get my speed up without feeling like I was dying. I still had a long way to go before I would consider myself a "runner" but my progress as satisfying.

Just as I suspected, about half an hour later Ryland showed up. I glanced at the clock. It was past curfew and everyone else had left the gym. I met his eyes in the mirror and hit the stop button on my treadmill.

"Don't stop on my account," Ryland said as he walked towards the weights. Headphones were dangling around his neck.

"I wanted to talk to you." My legs felt like jelly, but I managed not to look like a fool as I stepped off the treadmill.

"Why? Want to gloat in my face about how Luke is a better fighter than me and how you two ran off after class to do who knows what." He sneered.

The poison in his voice hurt me. "What? No! Wait, how did you know we left?"

"Luke was supposed to spar with me after dinner and he never showed. I figured it had something to do with you and you just proved me right."

My face burned red. "You shouldn't trick people like that."

"Whatever." Ryland shrugged and stretched his arms above his head.

I did my best not to be distracted by his muscles and failed. "Listen, I came here because I wanted to talk to you." He scoffed, but I kept talking anyway. "Haven't you noticed that something weird is going on here?"

"Yeah things have been plenty weird here since you showed up."

I flinched. My resolve was fading fast. Maybe Luke was right. Maybe I couldn't trust Ryland after all. He obviously had no intention of listening to me; he was too caught up in his own defeat to even care about the rest of the academy.

"You know what, fine!" I threw up my arms, ignoring how the metal plates latched on to my energy and trembled around us. "I was going to ask for your help, but you obviously don't care about anyone but yourself." I turned to storm off.

Ryland's hand closed around my wrist. "You're wrong. I do care. I care about you."

"Then why don't you show it?" My voice trembled.

"Because I don't want you to get hurt."

I didn't know what to say. I could see myself reflected in his eyes. I looked more like a confused child than a strong psychic in training. No wonder he thought so little of me.

"I'm no good at this "caring" stuff," Ryland admitted. "All my life I've trained to be the best I could be. My family accepts nothing but perfect. Since I've come here, I've constantly been in Luke's shadow. He is the star pupil. He's the multi-talented, a nice guy who everyone wants. Not me. I'm just the black sheep that no one trusts." He shook his head.

"So why do you spend so much time with Luke if you hate him so much?"

"I used to tell myself that it was because I wanted to learn his weaknesses." Ryland's voice lowered, and he avoided my gaze. "Now I know it's just 'cause I don't want to be alone."

What was I supposed to say to that?

"He's the only one who puts up with my bullshit," Ryland added. He turned from me, ashamed of what he had just revealed. "I guess, in some weird way, he's the only friend I have anymore."

Without hesitating, I stepped forward and hugged him tight, pressing my forehead against his back. He gasped and his hand drifted down to mine.

I wasn't going to tell Ryland that Luke was suspicious of him, that wouldn't solve anything. What I had to do instead was prove that he was innocent. The only way to do that was to find out who was really behind these strange events. If they had only begun since I enrolled, then it was my duty to solve it.

"I'm going to figure out what's going on here." I swore to myself, not caring that Ryland heard me.

"Bianca, I didn't mean for you to take it personally when I said that everything weird started with you." Ryland turned towards me and pulled me close. He smelled like soap and his face didn't have a hint of stubble.

I felt myself being pulled into his blue eyes. It was an almost dreamy state when our eyes locked. It was magnetic. "I didn't take it personally. It's the truth." My voice faltered as he cupped my cheek.

"You know what else is the truth?" Ryland's voice was low.

"What?" I whispered against his mouth.

"How badly I want you." Ryland kissed me hard and pulled my body against his.

I unraveled at his touch, throwing my arms around his shoulders and pressing myself against him. He groaned against my kiss and send a jolt of desire through my body. I arched my neck, and he kissed down my jaw and towards the center of my throat.

"Ryland." His name escaped me.

"What is it?" He asked, sucking on my neck softly.

"We shouldn't be doing this here," I gasped and pulled away slightly so I could look him in the eye.

"You're right. Shall we go somewhere more private?" Ryland grinned devilishly.

With one motion, he scooped me up in his arms and opened the door to the changed room that joined the gym. It was empty, as almost everyone changed and showed in the comfort of their own areas. Ryland moved to a bench, perching me on his lap and kissing my chest.

"I've been dying to finish what we started." He growled against my flesh.

I grinded against him, feeling his hardness. I wanted him so bad that my body was aching for it. I tipped his chin up gently so I could kiss him again. We went for so long that I thought I might suffocate against his lips, which wouldn't be a bad thing.

Ryland wrapped his arms around my waist. His hands moved up my shirt and explored the skin underneath.

I felt a strange ripple of energy, but I ignored it. He had sworn that he couldn't read my mind. It must have just been my imagination. When I parted my lips and deepened the kiss, the energy surged again.

I really hope she never finds out. She'd never look at me the same way again.

I heard his voice clearly in my head. I threw myself back and jumped off his lap. I blinked, staring at him, unable to comprehend what just happened.

"What?" Ryland's icy blue eyes were wide and innocent.

I stepped back, shaking my head and trying to calm my breathing. My hands trembled as I held them in front of me. I tried to speak a hundred times, but no words came out.

Finally, I managed four words. "Stay away from me."

∞

I packed my backpack and threw it over my shoulder. I didn't look back as I ran from the dormitories to the teleportation area.

There was a break in the fence right beside where students and teachers teleported.

I wasn't sure if it was an oversight or if someone at some point had tried to break in. Whoever they were, they would have been small. The fence was weighed down by overgrown weeds. I kicked the leaves back to reveal the small gap in the fence that I had noticed while helping Luke look for his tracking pin.

I sucked in my breath and wriggled through the gap, for once in my life I was thankful for my skinny build. On the other side there was nothing but a parking lot filled with crumbling concrete. When I looked back, much to my surprise, the illusion of an abandoned steel mill loomed above me.

I hesitated only a second before setting my shoulders and running off into the night.

I ran until I found a gas station on the edge of the city. By the time I got there, I was very out of breath. So much for progress. I paused, leaning against the pay phone to catch my breath before punching in Inspector Dolinsky's phone number.

No answer. I wasn't surprised that he wouldn't pick up for a random number.

"Shit," I sighed and then tried Daniel's cell. I was seriously lucky I had memorized his number. I couldn't recite any of my other friend's numbers, or even my dad's cell. He was the only one I could trust with this information now, anyway. My parents were still hypnotized into thinking I went to some fancy college on a full scholarship.

"Hello?" Daniel's voice was groggy. Thankfully, he was the kind of person who answered every call and even had a hard time hanging up on telemarketers.

"Daniel! It's me!"

Daniel gasped and his voice became clear. "Bianca? What's wrong? Are you ok?"

"Yeah, I think so. For now." I looked around to make sure I was alone. "I'm at a gas station near the freeway. Can you come get me?" I knew this was asking a lot of him. Daniel had his license, but he had always been a nervous driver.

"Anything for you." There was not a hint of hesitation in his voice.

I gave him the name and address of the gas station and hung up. It took all the strength I had not to ask him to leave me on speaker while he drove, but the collect call would already put a serious dent in his phone bill.

I slipped my cold hands into my pockets and sat on top of the propane tanks to wait. The night was cold for July. I surprised a shiver, wishing I would have thought to pack a sweater with the rest of my stuff.

I looked up at the sky. I couldn't see the stars or the moon through the clouds, which were reflecting a sickly orange hue from the industrial park's lights. Even the air smelled metallic and dirty here.

What was I thinking? This was crazy. I could only hope that Daniel got here before anyone else did.

The station clerk glanced at me a few times through the window but didn't say anything about my loitering. It didn't look like the kind of place that got much business at two in the morning and for that I was grateful.

About twenty minutes later, Daniel's beat-up old sedan rolled into the parking lot. He had bought it for literally two hundred dollars and hadn't used an entire tank of gas all year. The fact that he braved the interstate to come rescue me meant more than words could express.

I jumped off my perch and ran to him, hugging him as tightly as I could before breaking down in tears.

Daniel held me tightly. "Bianca, what happened? Did someone hurt you? Geez, your skin is like ice." He shrugged off his hoodie and wrapped it around my shoulders.

The warmth hit me immediately, and I slipped my arms into the sleeves. The fabric smelled like his favorite laundry detergent, and yes, we had been friends long enough that I knew what his favorite detergent was. I flipped up the hood and tucked my hair inside to stop it from blowing into my mouth as I talked.

"There's something going on at the academy," I said. "Something not good and I think it has something to do with me." I looked around to make sure we were alone.

Daniel mimicked my paranoid glances. "Come on, get in the car. Let's get out of here."

I slid into the sedan and buckled myself in tight. I couldn't stop shivering, even with his thick black hoodie around my body. "I tried to call your dad, but he didn't pick up."

"He's on the night shift this week," Daniel said. "He must have been busy." He kept his eyes forward and his hands and ten and two as he drove. His discomfort was palpable.

"I'm sorry I made you drive all the way out here." I said softly.

"Don't worry about it. I'm just going to take the back roads home. I almost lost my dinner on the freeway," Daniel replied. He shuddered. "So, what exactly is going on at the school?"

I shook my head, unable to believe the words that were coming out of my mouth even though I experienced them firsthand. "Someone is attacking students and teachers who teleport out of the academy and it all started happening after I came. I was attacked the other day by that creepy psycho that we met in the park." It seemed like a lifetime ago, but the memories were still fresh for both of us.

"What happened?" Daniel asked.

"We got him, and they took him in for questioning. Didn't your dad say anything about it?"

Daniel frowned. "I may know that psychics exist, but I am certainly not privy to the daily happenings inside the FBI," He said flatly and then shot me an apologetic glance. "Not that you would know that, sorry."

I smiled. "Don't worry about it. You have every right to be grumpy. I know how much you like your beauty sleep." We both laughed and reveled in how good it felt to just be together in the moment.

The road was dark and empty in front of us. Gravel picked up under the tires and pinged off the back of the car. It was relaxing. I blinked to keep my eyes open, only now realizing how tired I was getting.

"Nap," Daniel said, not missing a beat. "Let's get you back to my place and as soon as my dad is off shift, we'll figure out what to do next."

That sounded like a good plan. The reassurance was all I needed to allow my eyes to close and drift off to sleep.

I was jolted awake as the car came to a screeching halt and the horn blared in my ears. There was a man standing in the middle of the road. He had a trench coat on, and his face was unrecognizable as the headlights bleached out his distinguishing features.

"Crack head, get out of the way." Daniel honked the horn again, but the man didn't budge.

The ominous rumble of energy worked its way up my body. "He's no crack head, Daniel. We need to get out of here. Now."

Daniel paled and threw the car into reverse. He stomped on the gas and sped away backwards before coming to a complete stop. We could hear the tires squealing on the ground and the entire frame was trembling, but we didn't move an inch.

We both looked at each other. Daniel took his foot off the gas and let out a terrified sound.

The man moved both hands forward. He clenched his fists and the hood of the car buckled under his psychic force before being pulled forward like a toy to an electromagnet.

We both screamed; I wasn't sure who's scream was louder. Daniel unbuckled his seatbelt and fumbled to pull his phone from his pocket. It fell under the seat.

As I reached down to grab it, all four doors were flung open by some invisible force. It pulled me forward, but stuck tight because of the seatbelt around my body. The belt dug into my skin, leaving long red welts along my chest.

The force grabbed Daniel next. He flew out of the car and to the ground like a rag doll. He screamed, the force dragging him towards the man. The man, who had to be at least 6'5" and proportionally as wide, grabbed Daniel by his shirt collar and dug his thump into a pressure point. Daniel went limp; he was unconscious.

"Daniel!" I shouted, trying to release the seatbelt that had become jammed. "Shit, shit, shit!" I tugged at the buckle, but it was no use.

Seeing you want to do this the hard way, little girl, let's play a game.

A voice inside my head began speaking. It was that of a woman. She appeared alongside the man. A large-brimmed hat covered her eyes.

Return our partner and we will return your little friend.

The woman joined hands with the man, and they disappeared, taking Daniel with them.

CHAPTER TWENTY TWO

"Daniel!" I screamed and tugged at the seatbelt. When it refused to give, I growled with frustration and used my psychic power to rip the seatbelt free. I gasped and tumbled out of the car. I struggled to my feet and ran to where the couple had been standing, but they were long gone, and the psychic energy had faded. There were lines in the gravel where Daniel was dragged away.

Blinking away tears, I ran back to the car, grabbed Daniel's phone and tried his dad's cell. No answer again.

"Shit!" I threw the phone down in frustration. What was I going to do now? There was no one on the road and I could barely see in the darkness. Far away in the distance I could see the orange glow of the industrial park. I knew that it was my only option.

I pocketed Daniel's phone, pushed my sleeves back to my elbow and got in the car. Drumming my hands on the steering wheel, I gathered all my adrenaline-infused courage, turned the key in the ignition and shot off into the night.

I raced down the side roads while praying that a cop wasn't staked out around every corner. Thankfully, this part of town was dead at this time of night. I gunned the engine of Daniel's poor rusted car without stopping until I reached my destination.

I didn't want to attract attention to myself, so I parked on the side of the road near the academy's disguised island. No one would think twice about an abandoned car on the outskirts of Detroit. I grabbed my backpack and slipped through the narrow gap in the fence.

"Didn't think I'd be back here so soon." I muttered. It was surreal to watch the holographs morph around me and the academy come into view.

I ignored my aching feet and dashed across the grounds to the dormitories. The security guard at the front door was asleep as usual (how had he not got fired yet?). The wait for the elevator was mercifully short.

Once I got to the third floor, I wriggled through the doors and didn't stop until I reached Katie's door. I knocked as hard as I could.

There was a sound of scrambling feet and a shadow appeared at the peephole. She opened the door, rubbing her eyes. "Bianca? What is it?"

I pushed into her room and shut the door behind me. "Katie, I need your help."

Her eyes were wide and scared. "What happened?" She squeaked.

I struggled to catch my breath, seeing stars as my exhaustion finally caught up with me. Collapsing to the ground, I threw off the backpack and took a second to gather my thoughts before they all came spewing out.

"I was in the gym making out with Ryland, wait never mind that. Wait, no that's important. He freaked me out and I just snapped. I tried to run away by sneaking out. There's this little gap in the fence near the teleportation area. Did you know that? Anyways, I got out and met my friend at this old creepy gas station. Don't worry he knows about psychics. So, we start driving and get stopped by this weird guy. His powers were, like, so intense. He stopped our car! So, he and some lady kidnapped my friend and they say they won't give him back until we let that other Rogue go and I don't know what to do. I can't tell the Major cause then he'll know I ran away and I really don't want to get expelled, but I need to find my friend." My voice gave out and sobs took over me.

Katie was silent for a moment. She sat with me on the floor until I calmed down. "It's ok, it's ok." She repeated in a soothing voice.

"I'm sorry. I just didn't know where else to go." I cried, trying in vain to wipe tears from my cheeks.

"It's ok," She insisted. "I'm glad you came to me. It actually makes me feel useful for once. I can help you find your friend."

Relief washed over me. "Thank goodness." I dried my eyes. "Ok, how do we do it."

"I need something of his, it will help me visualize where he's being kept." Katie explained.

I pulled his phone out of my pocket. "How about this?"

Katie shook her head. "Electronics act weird around psychic powers. Do you have anything else?"

My hope momentarily deflated until I remembered I was wearing his hoodie. I shrugged it off, balled it up and passed it to Katie. "What about this? It's his favorite."

Katie smiled. "Much better." She held it in her hands and hugged it to her chest.

"Are you getting anything?" I whispered.

Katie opened her eyes and frowned. "No offense but I need total silence and concentration to do this properly."

"Oh," I said sheepishly and slid away from her on the floor. "Sorry. Go ahead."

Katie took a deep breath, closed her eyes and held the fabric to her chest tightly.

I watched her for a moment and then let my eyes wander around her room. It was decorated with posters of Scandinavian metal bands and weird art prints. Her bedding was black and there was a huge assortment of pillows on top. Some of them were strangely cute. Like in a creepy-cute sort of way.

I was itching to get up and explore, but I didn't want to do anything to distract her. Finding Daniel was the most important thing to me. It was probably the most important event I had ever experience in my life.

I glanced at Daniel's iPhone in my hand. The battery had jumped from 76% all the way down to 25%. It wasn't going to last much longer around all this psychic energy and Daniel's father hadn't called back. I turned it off, just in case I needed it later.

Fifteen long minutes later, a low hum filled the room. Nothing moved, but I could feel the frequency in my chest. With a gasp, Katie's eyes snapped open. "I see where he is. He's being kept in some sort of warehouse. Not far from here. His energy is close, and it seems stable, so they're not in a vehicle."

"How close?"

"Within ten miles," Katie said with absolute certainty. "To the west." She added.

I sighed and took the hoodie back from her. "Thank you."

Katie smiled. "Sorry I couldn't be more specific."

"Ten miles due west is pretty damn specific." I said flatly.

Katie shrugged. "I've done better. His energy is harder to track because he has no psychic talents. Normal people have much weaker energetic signatures."

"It's good enough for me," I said. "Thanks. Now I need to go find him."

Katie's eyes widened. "Uh, you're not telling me that you're planning on going alone are you?"

"Yeah. Why?"

"Do you really think that's a good idea after seeing how powerful those people were? I mean, they stopped a car. You should bring back up."

"Who's going to risk getting expelled to help me?" I sighed and let my head thunk against the wall.

A smile played around Katie's lips. "Well, I can think of two people."

∞

"I need your help."

Luke and Ryland looked up from their breakfast. Luke's expression became curious while Ryland's eyes darkened, and he looked away.

Ok, I deserved to be snubbed by him. Honestly, if it wasn't an emergency, I probably wouldn't be asking for his help anyway. I had no other choice. "Please, there isn't much time."

"What's wrong?" Luke asked, setting down his coffee.

I lowered my voice so I wouldn't be heard over the chatter of the other students. "Daniel's been kidnapped."

Luke gasped. "What? Are you sure?"

I nodded. "I really don't want to talk about it here." I glanced around. There were too many people, and I didn't want to be discovered before we even had a plan in place. "Please, help me."

Luke raised his eyebrows at Ryland who looked away. The blond was silent for a moment before sighing and releasing the tension from his shoulders. "Fine."

"You have some nerve asking me for help," Ryland whispered in my ear as we walked briskly down the hall. "After I opened up to you and you just left me there. What the hell was that?"

Luke was ahead of us. I kept my eyes on the back of his head as we weaved through the students, discretely headed to the training facility. It was empty at this time of day. We could talk there.

"I'm sorry, Ryland. Really, I am," I sighed. "I'm just kind of freaked out that I could hear your voice in my head when you touched me."

"What?" Ryland didn't believe me.

"You heard me," I said. "I don't know what happened, but it freaked me the hell out. What was I supposed to do?"

"Maybe get used to the fact that pretty much everyone here is weird by ordinary standards. Talk to me about it, ok?" Ryland said, his voice softened a fraction.

"Once we get through this, I promise we can have a proper talk about whatever," I pointed to myself and him. "Whatever we are. But right now, I need to focus on saving Daniel."

Ryland nodded.

I knew he wasn't happy, but I really didn't have time to dwell on it. Being attracted to two boys was never something I had dealt with before, especially on top of everything else that was going on. My best friend was kidnapped and something or someone was messing with the academy; my hormone driven emotions were just going to have to take a back seat until this was over.

The sounds of our boots clicking on the floor filled my ears. Once we were inside the training room, I told them everything. Every single thing that had happened since I freaked out, packed my bags and got my best friend captured.

"You never should have left the academy!" Ryland shouted. "Are you crazy? Those guys might have killed you."

"Easy," Luke raised a hand. "Let's not point fingers. What's important now is finding Daniel."

"If the Major finds out about this, we're all going to be in shit." Ryland crossed his arms over his chest. "Plus, that Rogue is under the custody of the FBI now. We have nothing to trade!"

"I know," I said. "I hate to drag you both into this, but I know you're the only ones I can count on for something this serious and you're probably they only two students here strong enough to take them on."

"Well, you're right about that." Ryland's ego could not resist the compliment. "Alright, beautiful. We'll do this. But you're going to owe us big time."

"Anything," I said with absolute honesty.

"A date." Luke and Ryland spoke in unison and then glared at each other.

"Fine, a date it is. One for each of you." With a smile, I stepped in between them to stop them from shooting daggers from their eyes. These boys weren't going to make my choice easily and now I had a deadline; there'd be no more playing hard to get once this was through. "Now, let's stop the flirting and get down to business."

CHAPTER TWENTY THREE

Luke and Daniel showed me to the closet with the technical gear that advanced students took out on unsupervised patrol. The large walk-in closet was filled with uniforms, belts, bags, weapons, and just about anything else someone would need.

My jaw dropped. "Wow!"

"Come on, let's be quick." Ryland stepped around me. "My security code will only keep the door open for five minutes before the alarm goes off."

We worked fast, gathering everything the boys thought would be helpful and then locked the door behind us. I slipped the night-vision goggled over my eyes. "Whoa, these are so cool."

"Don't turn them on in here, the lights will blind you. Night vision only." Ryland pulled them up onto my forehead. "These aren't toys."

"Yes sir," I said.

Luke stifled a laughed, and I smiled at him.

Once we finished packing, we crept out of the training facility and headed to the teleportation area. Luckily, it was early enough that the sun's position cast long shadows to disguise our movement. Most of the students were probably on their way to their first class now.

We stopped in the shadows and adjusted our backpacks. Under Ryland's suggestion, we packed light: first aid kits, light weapons and a few other gadgets that I hadn't been trained on. (Guess who was carrying the first aid kit? Me.) I was looking forward to the day that'd I'd be as skilled as my two partners.

Luke scanned the area again. "Aright," He said. "Where did your friend say that Daniel was taken?"

"About ten miles due west."

"Anything special noted? Landmarks?"

"She said it was in a warehouse. Some industrial zone."

"Well, that narrows it down," Ryland snorted sarcastically.

"You're really not winning points for our impending date, Ryland," I glared at him.

"It's enough. I'll aim for about ten miles from here and we'll see if we can sense any psychic activity." Luke said. "Ok, now for the important stuff. Transporting two people at the same time will be hard on me. I need you both to stay focused and think about Daniel."

"I can picture him already, Ryland mused. "The dork."

I bit the side of my cheek and ignored him. "Focus. Yes, no problem. Let's get going, we're wasting time."

"I don't think you three will be going anywhere."

We turned towards the voice. Professor Turner was standing their, looking strange in tactical clothes instead of his suit. He shouldn't be here. He was supposed to be teaching.

"What are you doing here?" I gasped.

"I should ask you that question. I missed you two at attendance and I thought something might be up. You three seemed to bring trouble wherever you go, don't you?" He sneered. His expression was different. He changed in a way that I couldn't quite pinpoint.

"Please sir, it's important." I said.

"I know what you're up to," Turner cut me off. "And I'll be damned if I let you interfere with my plans again." He brought his hands up and tossed Luke and Ryland back against the fence.

They grunted and pushed against his powers, but he had them pinned.

"Fuck off, Turner!" Ryland shouted.

With a flick of his wrists Turner drove them into the ground. "Shut up! Weak children like you must respect your teacher."

I swallowed hard. My legs were trembling. I gathered all my courage and lifted my hands towards Turner.

"I wouldn't do that, little girl," Turner laughed, and his powers brought my arms to my sides. He clenched his fists, and I felt my body being squeezed by the invisible force.

I gasped for air; my vision blurred as he pushed the air out of my lungs. "Please." My voice wheezed and gave out. The power let me go, and I crumpled to the ground, my body begging for oxygen. My backpack slipped off my shoulders and fell to the ground with a thud.

"I tried to do this discretely, but I suppose you've left me no choice." Turner grabbed my wrist. "Say goodbye to your boyfriends, you won't be seeing them again."

"Wait, please!" I shrieked and pulled against him with every ounce of strength I had left.

A moment later with a rush of energy and a pop, I was tugged from one space and teleported to another. The rush was unbearable, like the worst roller coaster ride of my life. Mercifully, it was over as quickly as it began.

I fell on cold, hard pavement. I tasted blood. Wherever we were, it was distinctly colder than the academy. The ground was wet as if we had just missed a rainstorm. I spat out blood and struggled to sit up.

Turner was standing over me, a knife in one hand. "Don't even think about using your powers on me, child."

I ignored him and tried to focus on my surroundings. I could hear faint sounds of water flowing. We must have been near a river; I could smell the distinctive scent in the air.

Turner hauled me to my feet and dragged me through a parking lot.

Looming in front of us were stacks of shipping containers; I knew where we were now. It was the same place we had been attacked by the Rogue.

"Where are we?" I demanded. "Is Daniel here?"

Turner laughed. "No, my dear. Daniel isn't here. I'm supposed to return you to my boss, but I wanted to have a little fun first."

The glee in his voice made my skin crawl. "No. Let me go!" I pulled against him, but he was too strong.

Turner raised the knife to my throat. "Don't make this harder than it already is, sweetie."

"Luke and Ryland will find me," I said.

Turner laughed. "Even if they do, they're no match for me. Let them come. I'll kill them on sight."

My blood went cold at the thought. He was right. He was incredibly powerful; I trained under him, so I knew better than anyone. Being a teacher, he probably knew all of Luke and Ryland's tricks.

I couldn't rely on them to save me. I had to save myself. With a guttural shout, I lunged at Turner, lashing out with my nails. At the same time, I grabbed his knife with my energy and pulled it out of his hand.

Turner threw me to the ground, wiping blood from the scratches on his cheek. "You're going to regret that one," He hissed as he threw his hand up in the air.

I felt the energy close around my throat. His psychic grip bound me and pushed the air out of my lungs. It was a good trick, and I knew why he didn't share this one with me during training. I tried to fight back, but without air I was fading fast. Not only was he draining my power, but I was losing consciousness at the same time.

I blinked, my shouts burning my throat. "Let me go!"

Turner chuckled and squeezed harder to prove his point. "You're not going anywhere. You're mine now."

With one last gasp, my vision blurred and went dark.

∞

It was hours later when I regained consciousness. I found myself tied to a chair in a dark room. It looked and smelt like an old basement. My first reaction was to shout, but I kept hold of my instincts. I seemed to be alone. The small room was empty, with nowhere for anyone to hide.

My hands were secured behind my back and handcuffed to the back of the chair. I strained but there was no give. I was going to have to do this with psychic energy. I let out a long breath to calm my nerves. I would be ok. I had trained hard. This was not going to be the end of me; I still had to find David, and no one, not even Jackson Turner would stop me.

"Ah good, you're awake." Turner's voice made me look up. He appeared with a pop in the middle the basement and was grinning smugly. "I was beginning to think maybe I squeezed too hard and didn't some brain damage."

I could see red-orange sunlight coming through the grimy basement windows; the sun was setting. I must have been out for at least ten hours. I was no biologist, but I knew that wasn't good for my health. "Luckily, I'm doing fine, all things considered," I said sarcastically.

Turner chuckled. "I always liked your spunky personality, Bianca. It's really too bad it had to be this way. In another life, you would have been a star protege."

I eased my energy towards the handcuffs, not wanting to give him the chance to pick up on the shift in the air. I gently began to pry at the metal, hoping to snap it with my mind. It was hard to work on anything I couldn't see.

"I still could be," I said to keep his attention focused on me. "Why capture me like this if I have so much potential?"

"There is a greater purpose for you elsewhere."

"But you said I was an amazing student. You cared about me!" I raised my voice over the sound of straining metal links. The distraction was working.

"Whatever feelings you thought I had were nothing but the fantasy of a little girl. I needed to get you to trust me." Turner sneered.

I had to admit that hurt. I confided so much in him and hell, even had a weird crush on him. He had been more than a professor to me. My heart twinged at the realization that everything I'd felt was fake. "So, it was all a lie?" My burning disappointment fueled my energy and the last link gave out. "You're such a liar!" I shouted.

Turner laughed, a full head back, shoulders shaking laugh. "Oh, I'm sorry, did I make you fall in love? Just a little? Pathetic."

I used his taunting to fuel my power. My hands were free, but my arms and legs were still tied with rope. I was going to need to distract him a bit longer. I tugged on the ropes with my energy and tried to undo the knot, but it was hopeless without seeing them. I'd need to use brute mental force again.

"No words left, little girl?" Turner began to pace back and forth in front of me. "Now that you're awake, I was hoping we could have a little fun before I have to turn you over."

"Turn me over to who?" The rope behind me was stretching; just a little more and it'd snap.

Turner opened his mouth to reply and then snapped it shut. "I'm not going to tell you, that would ruin the surprise."

The rope began to fray and unravel. This concentration of power was depleting my energy fast. The rope snapped and fell around me loose.

Turner spun around. "What was that?" His eyes wandered down my body to the ropes pooling at my hips. "Oh, you little she-devil!" He laughed. "Got me distracted, didn't you?" He raised his hand to me, and the ropes pulled together tightly. "Nice try."

Suddenly, there was a burst of energy in the room.

Luke and Ryland appeared. Luke was panting. Ryland had his daggers drawn and ready. "Let her go!" They shouted in unison.

Turner cocked his head to one side. "Well now, this is a surprise. I never thought you'd find her."

Luke threw my backpack down on the floor as if to answer the question. He must have tracked me using the belongings in my bag. "Sorry we took so long."

The ropes around me loosened again. "Darling, you'll have to forgive me. Let me take care of these boys and then we'll get back to business."

I gasped for air and resumed focus on releasing the ropes around my ankles. I had no time to be weak and tired. I had to free myself before Luke and Ryland got hurt

Luke ran to my side and Ryland lunged at Turner.

Turner held up his knife and clashed repeatedly with Ryland. He was as skilled at hand-to-hand combat as he was with his psychic abilities.

"Come on, let's get you out of here," Luke whispered and finished untying the knots around my ankles. He helped me to my feet, inspecting the rope burns and bruises on my body. "You'll be ok." He said. We had no time for pity; I'd just have to tough it out.

Ryland's eyes focused on the prize. He moved and dodged just as Turner made swipes for him with his knife. He was in the professor's mind now, anticipating every move like he had practiced with Luke.

Turner's frustration was burning hot. His movements became more sporadic as he tried to throw Ryland off. He reached out with other hand, grabbed Ryland with kinetic energy and tossed him against the wall. "Well," He panted, flicking hair out of his eyes. "I wasn't planning on having to kill you, but you leave me no choice."

Ryland grunted as he struggled to his feet. He attempted to move, but Turner's powers held his legs.

"It's so sad when a prodigy dies suddenly," Turner mused sarcastically and then tossed his knife.

"No!" I screamed and used everything I had to latch my energy onto the knife and stop it mid air. I clenched my fist, and the knife folded like paper and fell to the floor.

Turner looked at me. He seemed to be as surprised as I was.

I wasn't about to lose that advantage. "You taught me well." I smirked and then reached out. The handcuffs dangled broken on my wrists. I clenched my hands and held him; his power resisted, and we entered a psychic tug of war.

The deep hum filled my body. Every one of my nerves was tingling. My heart was pounding. My head ached. I would not let him go. I couldn't let him go.

Luke put his hands on my shoulder. "You can do it, don't let him win." He whispered in my ear.

Turner wrestled against me. "Let me go, you bitch!"

Ryland was released from the professor's hold. He tumbled to the floor and grabbed one of his daggers. I watched him from the corner of my eye as he silently crept behind Turner and drove his dagger deep into Turner's thigh.

Turner screamed and his power broke off. He clamped his hands around his leg, trying to slow the bleeding. I kept my psychic hold on him until he passed out from shock.

My hands fell limp at my sides. The room was deathly silent. "Is he dead?"

Ryland checked the professor's pulse. "No, he's alive. But he'll need to see a doctor." He looked up at me from the floor. "Remember what I said, psychics were teleportation powers are nearly impossible to catch. It was the only way." He wiped the blood off his blade. "Not that he would have hesitated to kill us."

My mouth tasted like bile. Deep down, I knew this would happen eventually, but I wasn't ready to see it.

Luke tied a tourniquet around Turner's leg and shook his head. "I suppose I should teleport him to the hospital and alert the authorities."

"What about Daniel?" I protested.

"We'll get to that. I'll only be gone for a few minutes." Luke rubbed his eyes; he could not hide his exhaustion. "It's better that we take care of him now than risk him waking up and getting away."

I looked at Turner. He was pale and cold but breathing. If we left him here, he'd either die or escape. Neither was an outcome I wanted on my conscious. "Fine."

Without another word, Luke grabbed Turner by his collar and disappeared in a ripple of energy, leaving Ryland and I to tend to each other's wounds.

CHAPTER TWENTY FOUR

"I'm sorry I dragged you into this." I winced as Ryland applied a medicated ointment to the rope burn on my wrists and arms. It cooled my skin instantly.

"Don't mention it." Ryland didn't look at me while he worked. "Thanks for saving my life," He added.

I blushed. "It was nothing," I said, trying to be modest.

Ryland's icy blue eyes met mine. "Why do you do that? Stop belittling yourself. What you did was epic. You stopped a knife mid-throw and crumpled it like paper. That shit was pretty cool." He grinned.

The sound of his laugh made my heart feel lighter. I smiled. "Ok, fine. You're right. It was cool."

"Took Turner by surprise too," Ryland said. "When this is over, I expect to see you sparring more often."

I looked at the broken handcuffs dangling on my wrists. "Yeah, when this is over." I tried to pry my hands out of the metal but failed. I wished that we would have found the key before popping Turner out. I summoned my energy to twist off the metal.

"No, don't do that." Ryland said, resting his hand on my shoulder. "We'll get them off the old-fashioned way back at the academy. We don't need you using any more energy." He grabbed some protein bars from his bag and tossed one to me.

I took a bite of the chalky chocolate-flavored brick and grimaced. "Ugh."

Ryland laughed and squatted down beside me. "Yeah, nasty, huh? But you need to eat or else you might pass out when we need you." He opened his bar and finished it in a few bites.

I forced down the rest of the bar and drank deeply from my water bottle. "Thanks."

Ryland sat down and nudged my foot with his playfully. "Anything for the girl who saved my life."

"You're not going to let that go, are you?" I asked.

"I dunno, do you think it'll get me a date when this is over?" Ryland's voice was low. He leaned in and kissed me.

I moaned against his lips, happy to lose myself in the pleasure and forget about the surrounding violence, even if it was just for a second. He pulled me into his arms, and I put a hand on his chest. Being with him felt so right, no matter how much I tried to deny it.

The pressure spiked in the room and Luke reappeared.

I pulled away quickly, but by the look on his face, he had seen enough.

"Alright, let's get moving." Luke said, not meeting my eyes.

"Wait, are you sure you don't need to rest?" Ryland said. "You've been popping in and out like crazy. You must be exhausted."

"I am," Luke said flatly. "But now is not the time to worry about it. We need to save Bianca's friend before something bad happens to him." He shouldered his bag. "I left Turner at the hospital. The authorities have been notified. If you want to help Daniel, we need to find him and manage the Rogues until the FBI shows up." He finally looked at me, but his expression was cold and business-like. "I noticed a cell phone in your bag. You can use it to call for back up as soon as we've found him."

"Why not call now?" Ryland asked.

"I was advised to scout the area first. If a bunch of agents start poking around, chances are good that whoever has Daniel will teleport out of there at the first sign of trouble. We need to be discrete."

Ryland nodded. "Ok, let's do this." He unceremoniously grabbed Luke's hand; neither of them seemed comfortable with the physical contact.

I pulled Daniel's hoodie out of my bag and held it to my chest. We'd need it to teleport to him. The scent of the fabric brought memories flooding back.

Luke held out his hand to me. "I need you to think really, really, hard. Focus on Daniel and nothing else. Transporting three people is going to suck."

I let out a shaking breath and took his hand in mine. "Ok. Let's go save Daniel."

∞

We reappeared somewhere outside again. I could hear dogs barking and an ambulance's siren in the distance. More empty warehouses, sprawling asphalt and overgrown weeds surrounded us. What was it with Rogues and living in squalor?

Luke stumbled and fell to his knees. His entire body was trembling after teleporting Ryland and me. I knelt beside him and put my hand on the center of his back; he was sweating and burning hot.

"Let Luke rest for a minute," Ryland shot me a glance and ignored Luke's half-hearted protest. "I'll scout around. There's a lot of psychic energy nearby. I can feel it." He set down his bag and crept off into the darkness.

If I closed my eyes and focused, I could feel the low rumble in the air. The power permeated the ground. "What do you think will happen when we show up without their partner to trade?" I wondered out loud.

"Don't worry about it." Luke shook his head. "I highly doubt they were looking for a fair trade, anyway. Rogues don't care about each other; they only care about themselves."

"So, they don't want him back?"

"If I had to guess, they want you alone a lot more than their little friend," Luke said. He grabbed a protein bar and forced down a mouthful. He raised his eyebrows and offered me a bite.

I shuddered. "No thanks. I'll wait for real food."

Luke chuckled. "Fine, have it your way."

Ryland returned a minute later. "The psychic energy is coming from that warehouse." He pointed across the parking lot. "I didn't see any scouts or guards, so we might just be able to catch them by surprise."

"They have a teleporter, though," Luke said. "She'll be hard to catch."

"As long as we get Daniel back, I don't care." I said.

Luke and Ryland both looked at me and then at each other.

"What?" I said after a beat.

Luke shrugged and Ryland shook his head. "Nothing." They spoke in unison.

"It's not nothing," I argued and jumped to my feet. "Why did you guys just look like that? What aren't you telling me?"

Ryland shook his head. "Honestly, nothing. But maybe you should reconsider keeping normal people as friends after this.

Obviously, it's dangerous for them. Why do you think the government keeps us a secret?"

I balled my fists and stomped my feet. Yeah, I know it was immature, but I was frustrated beyond words. "I refuse to let go of my old life!"

Luke put his hand on my shoulder. "Let's just get this over with. It's not the place to be fighting." He gestured around us to emphasize how out in the open we were. Thankfully, there was no one around the industrial area at this time of night.

"Fine." I double checked my boots to make sure I laced them tight and put my backpack on. "Let's go find Daniel, call for backup and then we can all go home." I grimaced when I realized I was referring to the academy at home; I had no time to dwell on it. We had to rescue Daniel. That was the only priority right now.

Follow Ryland's lead, we crept off into the darkness towards the warehouse. It was so quiet now. There were no lights on. Not even a raccoon rummaging in the garbage. We stopped at the back door. The lock was twisted and pried off and the door hung off the hinges at an awkward angle.

I gulped, remembering the psychic who had stopped the car with nothing but a flick of his wrists. He must have done this too. I gritted my teeth and tried to focus my thoughts. He was powerful, but so was I. I could twist metal and stop a knife in midair. I had been trained well by Ms. Blackwell and that traitor Professor Turner. I could take whatever was on the other side of that door.

Ryland whispered. "Ok, they wanted you. I suggest that you make yourself known. Be a distraction. Luke and I will take them by surprise."

I nodded.

"Do you still have that phone?" Luke asked.

"Yeah, it's in my bag," I said.

"Good. When we start the attack, I need you to dial 999."

I raised my eyebrows.

"It's the 911 for psychics," Luke said. "A line only for emergencies. I'll explain later. But they're expecting our call soon. They have a dozen agents on standby ready to teleport in here at a moment's notice."

A wave of relief washed over me. So, we wouldn't be going up against these guys alone. "Ok. Will do." I fished the phone from my back and slipped it into the zipper pocket of my leggings. I patted it just to be extra sure that it was secure.

"Be careful." Ryland's eyes locked onto mine for a fraction longer than they should have.

I wanted to kiss him, but I didn't. "Let's do this."

Before I could lose my nerve, I pushed open the door and walked in with my chin held high. I was not going to let them see how scared I actually was. I clenched my fists to keep them from trembling. The boys had my back; I reassured myself.

The warehouse was crowded and stuffy and dark. Shelves lined up in perfect formation, all of them cluttered with boxes and what looked to be small car parts. The dim lights barely illuminated the path before me. I had to rely on my senses more than anything. Now would have been a good time to have those night-vision goggles.

The lines of shelving stopped abruptly. My heart fell to the pit of my stomach when I saw what was at the center of the small warehouse: Daniel.

Daniel was tied to a chair with chains twisted tight around his body. I could see bruises where the metal had dug into his flesh. He was unconscious, with his head slumped awkwardly to one side.

I reeled in my instincts to make a more precise plan of action. I couldn't see anyone else, but that didn't mean they couldn't see me. They had been waiting for me. They knew I would come for Daniel; it was just a matter of when.

The handcuffs on my wrists began to tremble. I ducked down behind a shelf and watched the broken metal spinning around randomly like a broken compass. Before I could force them off me, I was tugged forward by my arms into the clearing. He wrenched my arms up above my head.

"Ah ha, it seems the girl came to play after all." The man who had kidnapped Daniel walked into the light.

The woman with the wide-brimmed hat followed him. "Finally. Don't you know it's rude to keep people waiting?"

I couldn't move my arms. The energy hummed through my body as the man's magnetic powers kept my wrists above my head. I kicked out my feet, but my efforts were in vain. "Fine, you got me. But let Daniel go! You have me, why else would you keep him?" I shouted as loud as I could to alert the boys.

The woman looked up as the man's power lifted me into the air. With the shadow of her hat gone, I could see her face. It took only a second for me to recognize her as the woman who snubbed me at the gas station that night with Daniel. Had she been watching me? Did she know who or what I was before even me?

The metal bit into my flesh. I let out a scream.

Suddenly, Luke appeared midair and grabbed me. His powers wrenched me free, and he teleported us back into the shadows. "Call 999. Stay safe. We got this."

My eyes met his as sounds of fighting filled the warehouse. Ryland was doing what he did best. With a pop, Luke vanished to reappear at his sparring partner's side.

"Where's the girl?" The man shouted. "Madam will be angry if she escapes again!"

I slunk back in the shadows and pulled Daniel's iPhone from my pocket. "Come on, come on," I urged as the load screen appeared. The screen flickered, and the battery fell to 5%. Damn psychic interference.

I prayed that the battery would last long enough for me to send our distress signal. I punched 999 and just as I went to tap the CALL button, the broken handcuffs began to spin again. That asshole was tracking me using his energy.

I tapped the CALL button and backed away from the fighting until I was sure that I was completely submerged in the shadows. "Hello, 999 emergency line. What's the situation?"

"I'm calling on behalf of Luke Herrington. We've located the Rouges." The sound of static made it hard to even hear myself.

"What's your location?" The man asked.

"I'm not sure," I admitted, glancing around the dark warehouse as if it would give me some answers.

"Hold on, we are trying to track you now. Stay on the line." The man's voice crackled before the phone went dead.

I threw down the iPhone in frustration; the screen cracked in a spiderweb pattern.

Our only hope was that they could track the signal or else we'd be done for. From the sounds of fighting, Luke and Ryland were not having an easy time. I had to step in, no matter what Luke told me to do. I wasn't about to let them get hurt.

I used my powers to wrench the broken handcuffs from my wrists. Snapping the metal too more energy than I expected. I wiped the sweat from my forehead and kicked them away. The skin on my wrists was raw and red, but at least that man couldn't use them against me anymore.

Luke and Ryland were locked in hand-to-hand combat. Ryland was using his telepathy to anticipate their enemies' moves and attack in perfect harmony. Even though I had seen in so many times, watching them fight was like appreciating a work of art.

I shook myself mentally to focus. My first objective was to get Daniel out of harm's way. They were fighting only paces away from his unconscious body. I glanced at the Rogue man and woman to make sure they were preoccupied before dashing to my friend's side.

I hid behind the chair and summoned my energy to break the chains. They weren't secured with a padlock; someone had fused the metal with psychic energy. Even though whoever did it would have been a crappy welder, it was enough to keep me busy.

I quickly found a weak point and put my hands on either side of the chain. I focused with all my might, directing my energy as it flowed from the base of my skull, down my spine and through my muscles towards the chain. With a ping, the chain broke and loosened.

Thankfully, the Rogues were busy with Luke and Ryland. Both sides were looking exhausted, and neither looked like they would give up anytime soon.

Daniel moaned as I dragged him away from danger. He was heavier than he looked; it must have been all that muscle mass he had put on lately. I made a mental note to compliment him on all those hours at the gym once we were out of this mess. Panting, I dragged his body outside the warehouse, leaving him propped up against the fence outside.

Daniel groaned and his eyes fluttered. "Bianca?"

"Hey Daniel," I whispered. "It's me. Are you ok?"

Daniel winced. "I guess."

"Don't move, you're hurt," I said. I put my hand on his cheek. "I need you to stay here where it's safe."

Daniel grabbed my hand. "Don't go. Please."

"I need to help my partners. Don't worry. I'll be back." I didn't hesitate, kissing his cheek and then dashing off back into danger.

If only past Bianca could see me now. I don't think she would have even recognized the woman I had become in only a few short weeks. I was no longer weak and wandering through life without purpose. I had found what

I was meant to do, and right now, that meant kicking some Rogue ass.

CHAPTER TWENTY FIVE

Ryland dodged the man's strikes, brandishing his daggers and shouting wildly. His opponent wielded a metal pipe like a sword. They dodged and clashed repeatedly. Luke was fighting with the woman; they appeared and disappeared at dizzying speed. Her hat had fallen off at some point, revealing beautiful auburn-red hair.

Deciding that the telekinetic guy was a better target, I summoned my energy, letting it flow through my body. I reached out and send my powers looking for small metallic objects. I gathered lost nails and screws in an invisible fist and then flung them at our enemy.

"Ryland!"

Ryland dodged just in time and turned to my voice. "Bianca, I told you to stay safe!"

The metal pieced pelted the man. He lost concentration and nearly dropped the pipe he held in his hand.

"When will you learn that I don't listen to instructions?" I laughed and used my power to pull the pipe from the Rogue's hands. With a flick of my wrist I bent it into a boomerang shape and sent it spinning towards him.

The man brought up his hands and stopped my weapon at the last possible second. "Nice trick, girly," He snickered. "But you'll need more than tricks to stop me."

Ryland was at my side with his daggers held high. "Alright, seeing how I'm not going to talk you out of this, let's get him."

I nodded, catching a glimpse of him out of the corner of my eye that made my body burn with desire. His face was like a marble statue; his eyes laser focused on his enemy.

Luke and the woman landed in the middle of our fight. Luke's energy was waning, but he held on desperately.

I felt a pang of guilt. He had done so much extra teleporting because of me.

Luke stepped back to my other side. We faced our enemies fully.

"Looks like you're outnumbered." I said, sounding braver than I felt.

The man and woman exchanged glances.

"What do you want with me?" I demanded, my fists clenched tight and my energy ready to surge at the smallest sign of trouble.

The woman laughed and shook her head. With a snap of her fingers her hat reappeared on her head. "It's not what we want. We're just following orders."

"Orders from who?" Luke demanded. His muscles were coiled tight, like a predator ready to pounce. Those with teleportation could disappear in a second and he wouldn't have a moment to lose if she did.

From me!

A voice filled my head. A woman's voice. I looked around wildly and Ryland's eyes met my own. He had heard it too.

Suddenly, a great pressure came down on us and I felt my powers bow to the will of the woman who appeared in front of us. We were clenched in invisible jaws, our entire bodies helpless and unable to move.

Bianca. I've been looking for you.

I gasped the sound was strangled away.

The woman's petite form radiated power. The air surrounding her was distorted, like the waves coming off the highway on a summer day. She wore a blank white mask that covered her entire face. Her hair was long and black, just like her long-sleeved dress. She hovered in the air, her bare feet just an inch from the floor.

I couldn't even look left or right, forced to face this woman. I felt a familiar tug of power; it was weak but noticeable. I used my mind to lock onto the flickering pulse of energy. She was blocking my power.

Listen to me. I have something important to tell you.

A crash echoed around us, but I could not look away from her. I saw lights and heard voices shouting. The psychic agents had found us at last.

The woman's frustration was undeniable. *No, I'm not losing you again. I cannot allow my incompetent underlings to fail again. Bianca! Come with me.*

I felt the tug and locked onto it, catching a glance where the feeling was coming from. A crystal dangled from her neck. The same necklace that I had seen being stolen from the museum. The energy radiating from the woman was most concentrated there.

Agents in black appeared, and the connection was cut. I fell to the ground, suddenly drained of all energy. Luke and Ryland tumbled down beside me.

"Stop where you are!" One psychic agent had a gun pointed at the trio.

Before anyone inched closer, all three of the Rogues disappeared with a flash.

My ears started ringing. My head was pounding. My stomach was in knots. I gasped for air and let out an ear-splitting cry, overcome with whatever had just happened to me.

∞

I woke up a few minutes later. I was wrapped in a gray blanket, propped up against the warehouse. Police cars and other unmarked vehicles filled the parking lot. Lights from the squad cars washed over me in alternating blue and red.

I felt numb.

"You're awake." Ryland came up beside me. He handed me a bottle of water.

I held it tightly but didn't drink. "What happened?" I asked, even though I remembered every tiny detail.

"They got away. Senior agents are investigating as we speak."

"Where's Luke?"

Ryland gestured to a squad car. "Resting. He might need to be on bed rest for a few days after that. He's completely drained."

I nodded. "Daniel?"

"He's safe. With agents now, I think."

Daniel's voice rang out over the buzzing activity. "Let me go. I need to see her!"

I didn't hesitate. In a flash I had dropped the water, flung off the blanket and started running towards his voice. "Daniel? Daniel!" I fought through the agents.

Daniel was sitting on the trunk of a car. "Bianca!" He jumped off to meet me.

We collided together, holding each other tightly.

"Thank God you're ok," Daniel said. He inhaled deeply. "I missed you. I was so scared."

I felt hot tears running down my cheeks. "Of course, I'm ok. I promised I would be. I'm so sorry I got you kidnapped."

There was a sharp intake of breath at my side. "Miss Hernandez, I need you to step away from the civilian."

I knew that voice. The woman who had hypnotized my parents. Agent Thompson. I planted my feet firmly, not letting her get any closer to Daniel. "Why? What do you want?"

"Only protocol for civilians that get involved with psychic matters. He won't remember a thing." She said coolly.

"No! Don't you dare touch him!"

Daniel held my shoulders. "I already know. You don't have to wipe my memory. I'm the son of Inspector Dolinsky!"

"It's not my decision to make." Thompson said without a hint of remorse.

Daniel shut his eyes tightly to avoid falling into her powers. "No. Call my father! I demand to speak to him. You can't do this!"

An agent grabbed my arm and pulled me away from my best friend. I had no energy left to fight back. I tried but my body failed me. "Let me go!" I grunted and pulled without success.

He was huge and strong. "Don't make this harder than it is. It's for the best." His voice was like stone.

Daniel backed into the car, his eyes closed, and his hands outstretched defensively. "Please don't do this. I'm not a risk. Talk to my father."

Agent Thompson closed the gap between her and Daniel. She moved his hands out of the way and began to talk in a soothing tone. "It's alright, Daniel. Everything is going to be fine. There was an accident. Nothing out of the ordinary."

"No!" I croaked.

"Stop this at once!" Inspector Dolinsky's commanded voice silenced the agents. He pushed his way through and pulled his son towards him. "How dare you try to wipe his memory!"

"It's protocol." Agent Thompson said.

Mr. Dolinsky gritted his teeth. "Don't talk to me about protocol. This is my son. He will be a useful witness, as one of the few civilians who understands our world." His voice softened. "Daniel, are you ok?"

Daniel blinked. His eyes weren't glassy like my parents had been. His memories survived, completely untouched.

I let out a sigh of relief and shrugged away from the giant agent who had finally loosened his grip.

Inspector Dolinsky shook his head and sighed. "This is madness. Let the agents clean this up and get the kids somewhere safe." He gestured to me and Daniel. "Come on, I'll give you a ride."

"You can't do this!" Agent Thompson shouted.

Daniel's father spun on his heel and looked down at her. "You can take it up with the Deputy Chief."

I didn't let my guard down until we were in the safety of Mr. Dolinsky's car. I sank down onto the leather seat and let the tension leave my body. In another time, I might have sobbed like a baby, but I did not even have the energy for that tonight.

∞

They didn't believe me.

I had been questioned half a dozen times and still no one was happy with my story. Why had I sneaked away in the first place? How did the Rogues know where to find us? Why was a psychic's normal son involved? Why did I complicate matters further by dragging my classmates into this? Why did Turner betray us?

Inspector Dolinsky told me that Turner's story was that he was innocent; he swore that he had intervened to stop us from getting hurt. Yeah, right. Ryland's testimony was no better, because he had a history of getting in trouble. Our only saving grace was that Luke was a star student, and they took him seriously.

Daniel was checked out at the hospital, but I was forbidden from seeing him. Daniel or any other normal person for that matter. I was to stay at the academy until the investigation was over and they could determine if I was safe from harm. I knew that meant that they didn't trust me.

I begrudgingly complied, for now, but I hadn't forgotten what that woman said.

Bianca. I've been looking for you.

Listen to me. I have something important to tell you.

No, I'm not losing you again.

Bianca! Come with me.

Who was that woman and what did she want with me? She had no hesitation about hurting people to get to me. Was I really that important? And why was she wearing the necklace that was stolen from the museum?

Too many questions and not enough answers. I swore to myself that I would find the truth, one way or another. I had come too far to give up now. I was so close to finding my purpose. I wouldn't give up now.

EPILOGUE

TWO WEEKS LATER...

"Good news, I heard from a professor that Ms. Blackwell has finally woken up from her coma. Once she testifies, it'll be all the proof we need to convict Turner."

I looked up from my notes at Luke. "What, like our testimonials aren't enough?"

Luke shrugged boyishly and pushed his hands into his pockets. "I know. But at least he'll be punished for what he did."

I nodded, absent mindedly tapping my pen against the coil of my notebook. Ethics class was a real bore with our new teacher.

"What's up?" Luke questioned as he sank down beside me on the couch. The common room was empty at this time of night. Every time we were alone, I ran the risk of melting into his arms again.

"Just looking forward to seeing my parents this weekend," I said, which was nearly the whole truth. I was also looking forward to seeing Daniel. He and I hadn't spoken since the investigation, which was filled with nothing but awkward and painful memories.

The administration had reluctantly agreed to let me off campus on a supervised visit even though the Rogues had not yet been captured. They weren't taking chances with my safety; I knew that this meant they wanted to keep an eye on me more than anything. I doubted that their concern for my wellbeing outweighed their distrust.

Luke nodded. "Yeah, same here." The Major had put even stricter controls on teleportation, so Luke had to wait for permission to visit his parents. Any secret teleporting off campus would lead to an automatic suspension, or worse.

I was very aware of how close he was to me. Desire pulsed through my body. His t-shirt was tight in all the right places, give me an excellent view of his sculpted shoulders and biceps. The thin white fabric contrasted with his dark skin.

Luke's breath hitched. He felt the pull between us too. His eyes softened, and he leaned in towards me.

I kissed him, craving a momentary reprieve from the stress I was under. I pressed against him, leaning back as he moved on top of me, his hands wandering every inch of my body as we kissed. His lips parted and his tongue brushed against mine.

I moaned against his lips, wrapped my arms around his back as he pushed his body against mine. I wanted to blend myself with him and forget about everything playing in the back of my mind. Right now, all I wanted was to be touched, kissed, loved, worshiped.

Luke's hand moved up my shirt to cup my breast.

My breath caught in my throat. "Luke, maybe we shouldn't be doing this here."

Luke eyed the security camera in the corner. "True." He smiled mischievously.

There was a pop of pressure and suddenly I found myself in a different room. A bedroom. We were on a bed with soft blue blankets and dim lighting. It only took a moment for me to realize it was Luke's dorm room.

My breath caught in my throat. I had never been with a boy like this before. It had always been a fumbling, nervous experience in the back of a car or an untidy rec room. This was so intimate. So private. So much better.

"Is this better?" Luke asked while his hand wandered up my inner thigh.

I nodded, not trusting myself to speak coherently. My heart was fluttering in my chest and a fire was burning within me, begging for his touch.

Luke kissed me, running his hands up my t-shirt and unclasping my bra. He removed the layers of fabric and lace until I was completely naked. His eyes grew wide and his voice went low. "You're beautiful, Bianca."

I clutched his shirt as he kissed me, his hands grabbing my breasts, moving down my body and to my core. His touches made me moan and writhe with pleasure. I lifted the hem of his shirt, feeling his hard, defined muscles flex in response to my gentle touch.

"Please, I want you." I couldn't wait any longer. I had craved this moment since the first moment we met.

Luke grinned, stripped down, and joined me under the covers. His hardness met my softness, and we became one.

Starting tomorrow, everything would change. I would not rest until I discovered what was happening in this academy and why that woman wanted my powers. I would not rest until I found the truth.

But for tonight, I was Bianca, a regular college girl with her crush and not a care in the world.

AUTHOR'S NOTE

Thank you for reading PSYCHIC SECRET (Psychic Academy Book 1). I have so much planned for Bianca, Ryland, Luke, and the rest of the cast in the coming months, so stay tuned!

If you liked PSYCHIC SECRET, please consider leaving a review on Amazon or Goodreads. This helps indie authors like me keep telling stories for readers like you!

If you're interested in getting news about upcoming releases, giveaways, book recommendations, and other great stuff, please consider subscribing to my newsletter!

NEWSLETTER: http://eepurl.com/gyM0wH

OTHER BOOKS BY SAMANTHA BELL

Psychic Academy Series (2019)

PSYCHIC SECRET (Psychic Academy 1)
PSYCHIC PRODIGY (Psychic Academy 1.5)
PSYCHIC LIES (Psychic Academy 2)
PSYCHIC TRUTH (Psychic Academy 3)

Stand Alone Novels

BECOMING HUMAN (2017)

ABOUT THE AUTHOR

SAMANTHA BELL is a writer, student, and self-diagnosed book hoarder. She has been living in her imagination as long as she can remember.

Support the Psychic Academy series and future projects by following Samantha Bell on social media!

FACEBOOK
https://www.facebook.com/samanthabellblog/

TWITTER
https://twitter.com/SamanthaWrites0

WEBSITE
http://www.samanthawrites.ca/

Made in the USA
Columbia, SC
20 June 2024